BILL "BOJANGLES" ROBINSON

DANCER

ARTISTS OF THE HARLEM RENAISSANCE

MEGHAN E. CUNNINGHAM

Cavendish Square
New York

Published in 2017 by Cavendish Square Publishing, LLC
243 5th Avenue, Suite 136, New York, NY 10016

Copyright © 2017 by Cavendish Square Publishing, LLC

First Edition

No part of this publication may be reproduced, stored in a retrieval system, or transmitted in any form or by any means—electronic, mechanical, photocopying, recording, or otherwise—without the prior permission of the copyright owner. Request for permission should be addressed to Permissions, Cavendish Square Publishing, 243 5th Avenue, Suite 136, New York, NY 10016. Tel (877) 980-4450; fax (877) 980-4454.

Website: cavendishsq.com

This publication represents the opinions and views of the author based on his or her personal experience, knowledge, and research. The information in this book serves as a general guide only. The author and publisher have used their best efforts in preparing this book and disclaim liability rising directly or indirectly from the use and application of this book.

CPSIA Compliance Information: Batch #CS16CSQ

All websites were available and accurate when this book was sent to press.

Library of Congress Cataloging-in-Publication Data

Names: Cunningham, Meghan Engsberg.
Title: Bill "Bojangles" Robinson: Dancer / Meghan Engsberg Cunningham.
Description: New York: Cavendish Square Publishing, 2017. |
Series: Artists of the Harlem Renaissance | Includes bibliographical references and index.
Identifiers: LCCN 2015036263 | ISBN 9781502610737 (library bound) |
ISBN 9781502610744 (ebook)
Subjects: LCSH: Robinson, Bill, 1878-1949. | Dancers–United States–Biography. |
Entertainers–United States–Biography. | African American dancers–Biography. |
African American entertainers–Biography.
Classification: LCC GV1785.R54 C86 2016 | DDC 792.8092–dc23
LC record available at http://lccn.loc.gov/2015036263

Editorial Director: David McNamara
Editor: Amy Hayes/Jill Sherman
Copy Editor: Nathan Heidelberger
Art Director: Jeffrey Talbot
Designer: Stephanie Flecha
Senior Production Manager: Jennifer Ryder-Talbot
Production Editor: Renni Johnson
Photo Research: J8 Media

The photographs in this book are used by permission and through the courtesy of: Michael Ochs Archives/Getty Images, cover; Keystone-France/Gamma-Keystone via Getty Images, back cover; Transcendental Graphics/Getty Images, 5; Library of Congress - edited version © Science Faction, 6; Hulton Archive/Getty Images, 10–11, (background and used throughout the book); Kenneth Alexander/Hulton Archive/Getty Images, 11; Publisher: Harmsworth Brothers/File:A Professional Pickaninny.jpg/Wikimedia Commons, 16; Universal History Archive/UIG via Getty Images, 18; NY Daily News Archive via Getty Images, 21; Afro American Newspapers/Gado/Getty Images, 25, 44, 46, 61, 76, 98, 106, 111; Hulton Archive/Getty Images, 31, 55, 69; Museum of the City of New York/Getty Images, 33; General Photographic Agency/Getty Images, 36; Everett Collection Historical/Alamy Stock Photo, 38; Cornell Capa/The LIFE Picture Collection/Getty Images, 48; Esther Bubley/File:1943 Colored Waiting Room Sign.jpg/Wikimedia Commons, 51; International News Photo/File:Jesse Owens and Bill Bojangles Robinson 1936.jpg/Wikimedia Commons, 52; 20th Century-Fox/Getty Images, 56; Archive Photos/Getty Images, 64; Fox/Getty Images, 71; Charles 'Teenie' Harris/Carnegie Museum of Art/Getty Images, 73, 79, 103; PoPsie Randolph/Michael Ochs Archives/Getty Images, 82; George Karger/Michael Ochs Archives/Getty Images, 84; MPI/Getty Images, 86; Movie Poster Image Art/Getty Images, 90; Mark Rucker/Transcendental Graphics, Getty Images, 92; Ralph Morse/The LIFE Images Collection/Getty Images, 95, 101; Credit TK, 96; George Konig/Keystone Features/Getty Images, 109; AF archive/Alamy Stock Photo, 113.

Printed in the United States of America

TABLE OF CONTENTS

Part I: The Life of Bill "Bojangles" Robinson

Chapter 1   7
Growing Up in the South

Chapter 2   21
Home in Harlem

Chapter 3   37
Gambling, Marrying, and Fighting

Part II: The Work of Bill "Bojangles" Robinson

Chapter 4   57
The Professional Tap Dancer

Chapter 5   77
The Famous Black Entertainer

Chapter 6   99
Tapping into the Twenty-First Century: Bojangles's Legacy

Chronology   116

Robinson's Most Important Works   118

Glossary   119

Further Information   122

Bibliography   124

Index   126

About the Author   128

PART I

The Life of Bill "Bojangles" Robinson

"Bill was a legend. Born within the shadow of slavery and dying at the middle of the twentieth century, the most glorious century of mankind, Bill Robinson was legend."

—Reverend Adam Clayton Powell Jr.

CHAPTER ONE
GROWING UP IN THE SOUTH

Bill "Bojangles" Robinson was born on May 25, 1878, in Richmond, Virginia. His given name was Luther Robinson. A southern city in the **antebellum**, or pre–Civil War, tradition, Richmond had been the seat of the Confederate government during the Civil War. It fell to Union forces on April 3, 1865. Shortly thereafter, Confederate general Robert E. Lee surrendered to Union general Ulysses S. Grant. Immediately after the Civil War, federal troops occupied Richmond as part of the **Reconstruction** plan.

RECONSTRUCTION IN RICHMOND

Robinson was born thirteen years after the abolition of slavery and the advent of Reconstruction. The federal government put Reconstruction into place to reunite the North and the South and to allow the Southern states to return to the United States. Two years after the Civil War, Congress passed the Reconstruction Acts of 1867, which laid out the official plan for Reconstruction.

Opposite: The poster for J. C. Lincoln's Sunny South Minstrels highlights the stereotypical activities portrayed in minstrel shows.

Robinson's parents were working-class blacks. They grew up in the shadow of the Civil War and lived in Richmond during Reconstruction. Robinson's parents were young adults during Richmond's occupation, which actually provided many opportunities for black citizens. Voters elected twenty-one black citizens to serve in the lower house of the Virginia state legislature. In addition, one black Virginian, John M. Langston, was elected to Congress. Unfortunately, the political rights of black citizens were short lived in Richmond. Despite the ratification of the Thirteenth, Fourteenth, and Fifteenth Amendments, segregation and discrimination would become the standard practice in Richmond.

In 1880, Maxwell Robinson, a machinist, and his wife, Maria, a choir director, lived at 915 North Third Street in Richmond with their two-year-old son, Luther. A few years later, the Robinsons had a second son named William. Unfortunately, by 1885, Maxwell and Maria were dead. The exact dates of their deaths are unknown, but it is certain that they died prior to 1885. That year, a fire destroyed all of Richmond's census and government records, including the Robinsons'. It is likely that they died from some kind of accident, rather than of natural causes. Even if census records had survived, there is no guarantee that there would be more information. Records of black Americans were not kept as carefully as those belonging to whites.

BOYHOOD IN RICHMOND

After their parents died, the two young boys went to live with their grandmother, Bedilia Robinson. She had been a slave in Richmond before the Civil War and was a strict, religious woman. In her house, the boys were subject to her authoritarian rules and discipline. As a Baptist, Robinson's grandmother forbade her grandchildren from dancing or even saying the word "dance." She even discouraged friendships with other children. Any friends that they brought around she identified as just a group of "street kid[s]."

Bedilia resented the responsibility of raising her grandsons. She actively fought to rid herself of the responsibility of the two boys in the Richmond court system. Bedilia Robinson's custody fight was brought before Judge John Crutchfield in Richmond's criminal court. "Justice John," as he was known, was famous for his fairness and concern for the city's orphans. At one point, the judge took in the boys until a suitable guardian was found, although who that guardian was is not clear or well documented. The judge's compassion instilled Robinson with a sense of respect for the law. This regard for the law would continue throughout his life—often in unique ways.

Despite the tense relationship Robinson had with his grandmother, she did give him the nickname Snowball. The name may have come from his extreme love of vanilla ice cream, but the truth is not known. When he returned as an adult to perform in Richmond, Bedilia attended his shows and called him by this nickname.

In the eulogy television personality Ed Sullivan gave at Robinson's funeral, he described the formative relationship Robinson had with his parents and grandparents. Even in their absence, "Bill Robinson never forgot the grandmother who had raised him, and that grandmother had been a slave. And so every honor that he received throughout his lifetime, he accepted as an honor to his mother and father, to his grandmother, and particularly to those of his race."

ROBINSON DANCES

School did not play a large role in Robinson's life. He never learned to read and write—not even the sheet music he used as a professional dancer. Through much of his career, Robinson's second wife, Fannie, organized his music and helped him learn lines and music. Rumor has it that when Robinson attended school as a young boy, he had a hard time getting along with the other children. This was, in part, due to his given name, which

MINSTREL SHOWS

Minstrel shows are a distinctly American theater form. They began on Southern plantations with semi-professional black bands. By the early 1800s, minstrel shows included white performers who imitated black people by covering their faces with burnt cork. Today, this practice of dressing in blackface is highly offensive. Minstrel shows had an established pattern of three acts. The shows relied heavily on white perceptions of black culture. They used stock characters like the slave, the "dandy," and the "mammy." The stereotypes were often unflattering. These shows presented caricatures of blacks as lazy or "simple," another way of calling someone stupid. These depictions were not always intentionally cruel and could even be sympathetic. However, they lacked any real understanding of black people. The caricatures were highly racist.

The Civil War changed the structure and nature of minstrel shows. Any sympathy white Southerners had for former slaves was gone. Whites blamed blacks for the war and its effect on their lifestyle. A lot of common stereotypes, like **Jim Crow** and **Uncle Tom**, began to pop up in Southern minstrel shows. Eventually, black performers were forced to use blackface. It was a way of removing the humanity from the character they were performing. Gradually, **vaudeville** replaced the minstrel show.

Opposite: This performer is in the typical blackface makeup used in minstrel shows.

Growing Up in the South

he claimed was Luther. After a fight with his younger brother, William, Robinson assumed the name William for himself. He decided that his younger brother would now be called Percy. While there is no way to confirm this story, it does illustrate two of Robinson's persevering attributes: he had a big temper and a desire to control, or have the upper hand in, his relationships. Aside from the name, Robinson's brother never played a large role in his life.

Robinson and his friends did not spend much time in school. There were no child labor laws in the late 1800s. Since money was hard to come by, he and his friends skipped school and found various ways to make money on the street. In fact, the street is where Robinson met most of his friends.

Lemmeul V. "Eggie" Eggleston was one of Robinson's closest friends while in Richmond. Eggie was four years younger than Robinson, and they often found work together. Sometimes they shelled peas at the Jefferson Market, which was the main shopping area in Richmond. Robinson and Eggie also worked as **bootblacks**, or shoe shiners, for five cents a shine. Robinson's most famous odd job was dancing outside of the Ford Theater. Before the minstrel shows, he and Eggie entertained people on the street. Although African Americans were the subjects of these minstrel shows, the theater did not allow Robinson and Eggie inside. Black people were not allowed to attend the performances.

George H. Primrose sponsored some of the biggest minstrel shows that came through Richmond. Primrose was an Irish minstrel man who performed the **soft-shoe** and Irish step dance in blackface. However, he did not use a fake dialect, which was common among other blackface performers. Even though Robinson never saw Primrose's show, the entertainer left an impression on him. Robinson incorporated Irish step dancing into his performances and named Primrose as an early influence.

For Robinson and Eggie, it was natural to dance when their bootblack business was slow. Eggie danced the soft-shoe and

Robinson danced a minstrel specialty called the **buck-and-wing**. The buck-and-wing was part jig and part "chicken wing." To perform the chicken wing, Robinson would hold his neck still and flap his arms and legs about as he danced, resembling a bird. Both Robinson and Eggie danced without the aid of music, although they did write some of their own songs. Despite the fame that Robinson eventually achieved for **tap dancing**, neither he nor Eggie dreamed of making a living by dancing at the time. For both boys, it was simply a way to earn more pennies when business was slow. Eggie recalled later that if he earned more than Robinson,

LYRICISTS

Eggie and Robinson composed this song to provide background music for their dancing. The lyrics and music added depth to the sounds they made by tap dancing.

Kid had a cow
Cow had a calf
Sold the cow for seven-and-a-half
Then we went down the river
But we couldn't get across
Paid five dollars for an old gray horse
Now the horse wouldn't pull
So we sold it for a bull
Bull wouldn't holler
So we sold it for a dollar
Dollar wouldn't pass
So we kicked in the grass
There comes somebody …

Robinson would simply take the difference to make it even—he always wanted the upper hand.

Robinson's childhood working odd jobs and dancing is likely how he earned the nickname that would follow him his entire life. According to Eggie, he earned "Bojangles" as a nickname after an incident with a misappropriated beaver hat. The beaver hat came from a hat-making and hat-repair shop owned by Lion J. Boujasson. Due to the difficulty in pronouncing his last name, the neighborhood children called him Bojangles. After acquiring the hat, Robinson and Eggie had a hard time selling it. It became a joke on the street. "Who took Bojangles's hat?" someone would ask. The response came: "Why, Bojangles took it." Then they would point at Robinson. Somehow, the name stuck.

There are other stories about how Robinson inherited the name Bojangles. Some sources say it signifies a scrappy fighter, which also fits Robinson's early life. He wasn't afraid to give in to his temper and fight other boys. Other sources say that Bojangles was a Southern term for mischief, which would also fit Robinson. Despite its unknown origin, the entertainer confirmed that he got the nickname in Richmond. The nickname lives on today. Bojangles is a synonym for an excellent dancer.

As the story of the nickname suggests, Robinson and his friend often fell into trouble. The two friends needed to eat, but they didn't always want to spend their money on food. Robinson and Eggie often stole bakery toss-outs, plums, apples, and even whole fish. According to Eggie, one time they acquired a bag of peas that was "lying around" and the police chased after the two friends. At the police station, Robinson danced up and down the stairs. While the police were enthralled watching Robinson dance, Eggie ran away—and eventually Robinson ran as well. Little did the Richmond police know that Robinson would one day become famous for his stair dance.

Robinson and Eggie continued to dance together in Richmond. They eventually connected with a white boy named Lemuel Gordon

Toney, known as "Tots." Toney loved minstrel shows and baseball. Most of all, he wanted a way out of Richmond. By his teenage years, he was staging blackface shows for local Richmond churches. Toney heard about Robinson and Eggie and their performances outside the Ford Theater. After watching them, he saw that the talented Robinson could be his ticket out of Richmond.

ROBINSON GOES TO WASHINGTON

Toney created a blackface act based on his experience at the Ford Theater, but he also wanted to incorporate a gimmick: **pickaninnies**, or "picks" for short. A pickaninny was a small black child who could entertain by singing, dancing, telling jokes, and looking cute on stage. He approached Robinson and Eggie about going on the road as picks. None of the three boys had any money to actually set out on the road, however. That changed one night when a club patron asked Toney to bring in some champagne. He handed Toney twenty dollars. Instead of buying the champagne, Toney took the money and went to find Robinson and Eggie. He wanted to use the money to get to Washington, DC.

The three boys set off for the train station, but Eggie turned back. He was uncomfortable leaving his family. Toney and Robinson grabbed the truss rods of a boxcar and climbed to the top. Toney slipped. The train was traveling at 35 miles per hour (56 kilometers per hour). Luckily, Robinson managed to catch hold of his leg, saving Toney's life.

Robinson wasn't even twelve years old, but his childhood essentially ended when he left Richmond for Washington, DC. School, or any formal education, was no longer a part of his life. He was solely responsible for his food, shelter, and livelihood. Although it was only about 110 miles (177 km) away, Washington was far enough away for Robinson to start a whole new life.

At first, Robinson's life in Washington closely resembled his life in Richmond. He and Toney picked up odd jobs around

A PROFESSIONAL PICKANINNY.

A pickaninny poses for the camera in his early days of performing.

the city, usually dancing at beer gardens. Neither boy actively pursued dancing as a career; it was just a way to make some extra money. Toney wanted to be a professional baseball player. He spent time in Baltimore, Maryland, with the Orioles. At the time, baseball was still segregated. Only whites could play on the team. Robinson knew getting a job with Toney and the Orioles wouldn't be possible. Instead, he got a job rubbing down sweating horses at Bennings Racetrack.

While working at the stables, Robinson dreamed about becoming a horse jockey. Being a horse jockey would have been a good career for him. It probably would have suited him well. In the late 1800s, most jockeys were black, and Robinson had a slight build, perfect for a jockey. More importantly, Robinson enjoyed the characters at the racetracks—and the gambling. Beginning with his days at the racetrack, Robinson would forever be known as a gambler, just as he would become known as a dancer and entertainer.

Eventually, Robinson lost his job at the racetrack. For a while he had to steal bread and milk to survive. Although he was stealing out of necessity, Robinson had an honor code. He drank the milk right from the bottle on the doorstep. That way, the owner would not lose his or her bottle deposit. Robinson also tried selling newspapers, but eventually he returned to dancing on the street. This time, the dancing was different. He formed a partnership with a white boy who sang while he danced. They mainly performed in order to drum up newspaper sales. His music partner was none other than Al Jolson, who would also become famous for vaudeville, singing, and dancing.

Eventually, Robinson reconnected with Lemuel Toney. They were able to break into the vaudeville circuit. Toney was hanging around the Baltimore Orioles when he was discovered by George Primrose, the owner of one of the minstrel shows that had traveled through Richmond. Primrose was also an avid Baltimore Orioles fan. He put Toney in the Primrose and West shows.

Al Jolson became famous for the first "talking" motion picture, *The Jazz Singer*

Toney assumed the name Eddie Leonard and used his influence to help Robinson get his first big break. **Impresarios** Whallen and Martel hired Robinson to play a pickaninny in their show *The South Before the War* in about 1892. The show, which was advertised as the greatest production of the century, traveled up and down the US Eastern Seaboard. Robinson stayed with it for about a year, serving as a "pick" for Mayme Remington, a white female vaudeville star. Robinson earned fifty cents a night for his performance. He provided backup and participated in the grand finish of the vaudeville act.

Unfortunately, Robinson's first big break was short lived. As he began to grow, he was no longer cute enough for the role. Although it was only for a few short years, the pick chorus was Robinson's first big professional job. It gave him the opportunity to collaborate and perform in an ensemble with other black men. This job laid the foundation for Robinson's career in show business.

A NEW DIRECTION

During the five years or so after playing in *The South Before the War*, Robinson didn't have consistent work. He traveled around quite a bit. In 1898, he returned to Richmond and tried to join a black regiment to fight in the Spanish American War, but he didn't make the outfit. He wasn't able to serve as a regular solider, but he did accompany the outfit as a drummer. Other accounts of Robinson's life state that after becoming a pickaninny in 1892, he worked his way to New York City in traveling shows. Either way, by the turn of the century, Robinson was dancing and entertaining. By then he was dancing in Minor's Theatre in the Bowery and in dinner shows on Brooklyn's Coney Island.

He had made it out of a segregated city and was ready to seize the opportunities that New York City and the North had to offer. Although Robinson would never live in Richmond again, he would visit and be incredibly generous to his birthplace.

CHAPTER TWO

HOME IN HARLEM

Although Robinson had arrived in New York City by 1900, at the age of twenty-two, he didn't immediately take up residence in Harlem, nor did he gain immediate success. Many argue that Robinson was not discovered until he was nearly fifty years old and debuting on Broadway. However, others claim his fame began to grow as soon he moved to New York. From the turn of the century through the **Harlem Renaissance**, Robinson experienced several good breaks. He joined the vaudeville circuit with a partner and debuted as the first black solo entertainer there. He also invented his own dance and performed on Broadway.

Robinson's arrival in New York coincided with what is now known as the **Great Migration**. The Great Migration was an exodus of blacks from the South. It was a precursor to the Harlem Renaissance in New York City. Many Southern blacks wanted new economic opportunities. They headed north to find new job opportunities instead of **sharecropping** or tenant farming, which was all that was offered in the South. Sharecropping was

Opposite: In the 1920s, a typical street corner in Harlem was a lively place full of local businesses and residents.

a system of farming common on large farms or plantations that was prevalent in the South. The farmers were essentially treated as slaves. Once World War I began, there were fewer immigrants from Europe coming into the northern cities, and thus there were plenty of job opportunities for blacks. In addition to the economic opportunities, African Americans had new ideas about how to live their lives. Many former slaves were growing older and passing away. The new generation was less content to be subordinate and accept the few opportunities that white society allowed them.

HARLEM RENAISSANCE

The Great Migration produced a burgeoning population in many northern cities, including Detroit, Chicago, and New York City. As the black population began to swell in the North, Harlem was on its way to becoming "the Black Capital of the World." The physical neighborhood of Harlem was originally planned as a "suburb," or a neighborhood for wealthy whites. It was developed in an old Dutch farming community called Haarlem. The developers overestimated how many white residents wanted to move north within the city. With townhouses and apartments sitting empty, the black population of Manhattan—which had tripled between 1890 and 1910—began taking up residence in Harlem as landlords reluctantly began to rent to them. Oftentimes, the rents were inflated and buildings weren't maintained. Early in the migration to Harlem, however, only wealthy blacks moved there. By 1910, ordinary black establishments and businesses began to appear in Harlem and with them, a middle- and working-class population. African Americans owned and operated their own businesses. They also began to write and entertain not just for whites, but to represent their own distinct culture.

The Harlem Renaissance was not just about the physical place. It was also about what it represented. The Harlem Renaissance meant liberty and artistic expression for black intellectuals.

Black artists, writers, and entertainers converged on the area. They created literature and other materials that were distinctly non-white. The first phase of the Harlem Renaissance began around 1917. It was capped off in 1923 with the publication of Jean Toomer's *Cane*, a unique prose poem. The second phase occurred between 1924 and 1926. It was marked by interracial collaboration between white patrons and black artists, such as in Zora Neale Hurston's writing. The third phase stretched from 1926 through 1935 and the Harlem Riot. Robinson's famous stair dance was part of the first phase, though his official "big break" did not occur until the third phase of the Harlem Renaissance.

One of the enduring artifacts of the Harlem Renaissance is an anthology of essays, poems, art, and songs by black artists titled *The New Negro* and edited by Alain Locke. The concept of the New Negro represented and rallied the black individual who would no longer submit to discrimination and racial segregation. In the anthology's title essay, Locke wrote of a new consciousness in the wake of the Great Migration and the talent descending on Harlem. He recognized the tradition of black art in music and folk art. He called for a new wave of artistic creation. The biggest challenge for black artists was to create distinct and unique works that also represented the African American experience. Robinson took up the challenge through his dance and entertainment.

BEGINNING IN NEW YORK

Robinson's life in the early 1900s included a lot of traveling and transition. It is hard to get a clear timeline of where he was performing and when. Around the year 1900, he and his dance partner, Theodore Miller, performed regularly at the exclusive Douglass Club. The Douglass Club shows a lot about the culture in which Robinson performed. The club was a place where wealthy whites "slummed." Its wealthy white patrons liked the opportunity to see "exotic" performers and let loose. Whites often saw blacks as exotic and exciting. While whites were entertained, the arrangement also afforded black entertainers more opportunities. The black entertainers who performed at the Douglass Club arrived after completing their gigs elsewhere. At the club, they performed again for tips. The tips were generous enough that this was attractive for the entertainers. Clubs were an important venue for the Harlem Renaissance and for Robinson's career. In fact, Robinson regularly performed in clubs, often several shows a day, throughout his career—no matter how famous he became.

Douglass Club patrons began to notice the young Robinson when he performed with Theodore Miller, but they were impressed with Robinson's singing, not his signature dance moves. Audiences finally took note of his dancing when he challenged Harry Swinton, the star of *In Old Kentucky*, to a dance off. *In Old Kentucky*, a vaudeville show, sponsored and hosted a dance competition every Friday night at Brooklyn's Bijou Theater. The contestants were only allowed **stop-time** banjo accompaniment. They danced against each other until all but one were eliminated. Swinton always danced against the winner.

Swinton was a very talented dancer. Many of Robinson's buddies warned him about Swinton's talent. Robinson took on several rounds of dancers before he got to Swinton. When he won the competition and beat Swinton, Robinson received additional publicity. He became the new person to beat at buck-and-wing dancing.

ROBINSON AND COOPER

As a black man, Robinson couldn't work in white vaudeville on the preferred Keith circuit which was a group of the most well-known vaudeville theaters, without a partner. In the summer of 1901, Robinson found dance partners who helped him break into the circuit. He began to work wherever and with whomever he could. Some of his partners included Bert Williams, George

Young Robinson dances with his trademark smile.

VAUDEVILLE

In Old Kentucky featured white actors and black musicians and dancers. The show included a melodramatic love story. It featured such gimmicks as a villain lighting a bomb under his enemy and an elaborate racing scene with real horses and a pickaninny band. Friday nights included the special feature buck-and-wing dance contest. Harry Swinton was the star dancer at the time and the dancer to beat in the weekly contest.

In 1900, *In Old Kentucky* was a new type of entertainment. It took the form of a traveling show. The minstrel show was no longer in its prime, but performers like Al Jolson performed in blackface well beyond the 1920s. In contrast, *In Old Kentucky* was categorized as vaudeville. Vaudeville, which is a precursor to the modern American musical, contained some components of minstrelsy, but was an entirely new format. A vaudeville performance didn't necessarily have one continuous storyline but a series of unrelated acts grouped together. A show could have acts with dancers, tap dancers, and singers. In fact, the vaudeville circuit might be more aptly considered the early twentieth-century equivalent of the modern American network TV circuit (*Good Morning America, The Tonight Show*, etc.). The only way an entertainer could be guaranteed mass exposure was to join a vaudeville circuit. Robinson became famous on the vaudeville circuit and for many years would strive to get the top **billing** for a show.

Walker, and Johnny Juniper. In 1902, Robinson and Juniper were touring together when George W. Cooper, a well-known black vaudevillian, requested Robinson for his partner. Robinson joined Cooper at his request. The partnership meant he began touring on a more renowned circuit. Changing circuits alone guaranteed Robinson more security and steady performances.

Unfortunately, Robinson lost his autonomy when he became part of Cooper's act. When he began dancing with Cooper, he was no longer the head of the team, as he had been with Juniper. With Cooper, Robinson had to play the fool, or comical character. Cooper got to play the straight man, or serious performer. Robinson was not allowed to dance, and he had to wear a comical outfit. His costume was similar to a clown's outfit and included a tutu worn over long pants. Cooper wore a suit and tie. Robinson was also expected to provide other comedy. He used his lips to make noises, like impersonating a mosquito or a trombone. Robinson's early partnership with Cooper began a career-long struggle against playing the Uncle Tom character or buffoon. Although he began his vaudeville career playing the buffoon, Robinson never performed in blackface.

Cooper and Robinson toured on the Keith circuit with regular bookings—something that black performers were rarely guaranteed. Cooper became a valuable mentor for Robinson. Robinson began earning $100 a week on the circuit, and he was guaranteed twenty-six weeks of employment in a year. On January 10, 1903, the duo officially became "Cooper and Robinson—Comedians." Their popularity began to grow. Each year they debuted a new act and played at all the leading vaudeville houses.

Over the next decade, Robinson's life changed in several ways. First, in 1907, he married his first wife, Lena Chase. Next, during this ten-year period, Cooper and Robinson continued to expand their act, which began to focus more on their dancing. Reviewers took notice. On May 14, 1912, a review in the *Denver Tribune* stated, "Both Cooper and Robinson are the genuine article and their chuckling guffaws, pigeon wing steps and cachinnating songs are a real vaudeville entertainment." At the time the article appeared, Robinson was no longer the second fiddle in the duo. He no longer had to wear comical clothing, like his clown-tutu outfit, or play the buffoon. Critics also took note of his dancing talent.

A few years later, in 1914, Cooper and Robinson performed their last show together at the Olympic Theater in Des Moines, Iowa. There are several theories about why the partnership ended. The most likely scenario is that Cooper planned to marry a white woman, a circumstance that would force him out of vaudeville. The prejudice of the time did not allow a black man to be married to a white woman and perform on the stage. So, in 1914, Robinson was again in need of a new partner, but his performances had guaranteed him a place in vaudeville as a leading black entertainer.

JUST BOJANGLES

Cooper and Robinson's breakup allowed Robinson the opportunity to become a vaudeville star in his own right. While Robinson had not performed in blackface, he had followed the "two colored" rule. This rule meant that two blacks had to perform together. It was a rule that white vaudeville and the Keith circuit required. Now that he was no longer part of a duo, Robinson wanted to move beyond the discriminatory rule. He wanted a solo act with complete control over his performances. He pitched the idea to Marty Forkins, the man who would manage Robinson's career. Forkins was an Irish Chicagoan with a law degree from the University of Notre Dame. When he met Robinson, he was an established and successful manager. His clients included Fred and Dorothy Stone and Will Rogers. More importantly, he knew how to market his clients. Forkins took a risk by representing and managing Robinson—the first black solo act in vaudeville.

Robinson's solo career began modestly, as the dance instructor at the Marigold Theater in Chicago. At the Marigold, he taught and worked alongside the chorus girls in residence. He occasionally performed on his own. Robinson stayed at the Marigold Theater for about a year. Then he began to perform at small theaters in Chicago and the Midwest. Within three years, he was back on the Keith circuit as the first solo black vaudeville entertainer.

As Robinson gained more notoriety on the circuit, the United States entered World War I in 1917. This gave Robinson a new performing opportunity. Suddenly, he had the chance to perform for the US troops. The US War Department provided travel expenses and lodging to encourage entertainers to give shows for the troops. Robinson took advantage of this and gained more exposure as a new solo artist. In addition to the positive publicity, Robinson had great respect for the military. He thoroughly enjoyed performing for their benefit. Robinson continued performing for the benefit of others throughout his life. He also kept the letter of commendation he received in 1918 from the United States War Department for his entire life. Robinson proudly collected tokens of appreciation during his lifetime. As a solo entertainer and a black man, Robinson took advantage of every opportunity to market his distinct brand of entertainment.

When the first phase of the Harlem Renaissance was kicking off in 1917, Robinson established himself as a tap dancer in vaudeville. He marketed himself by performing for troops. He then solidified his fame when he introduced his world-renowned stair dance. This happened in 1918 at the Palace Theater on West Forty-Seventh Street and Broadway in New York City. The Palace Theater was the showplace of the Keith vaudeville circuit. Robinson was one of three black performers to play at the Palace Theater during World War I. To perform the stair dance, Robinson needed the stage to have steps or stairs. The stage at the Palace Theater had a set of four steps on either side of the stage. They allowed performers to go down into the audience. The first time Robinson performed the stair dance, he saw some friends in the audience. He improvised and danced down the staircase to greet them. The audience was enamored with his easy dance up and down the stairs. The introduction of the dance would always be linked to New York City and the Harlem Renaissance.

LIFE IN HARLEM

Aside from the more formal Palace Theater, one of the most famous entertainment venues associated with the Harlem Renaissance was the Cotton Club. In 1920, gangsters opened the club in Harlem on 142nd Street and Lenox Avenue. From 1923 to 1936, it was one of the hotspots for black entertainers and white patrons. If you were white, it was the coolest place to go for entertainment. If you were black, it was the best show in which to perform. As a white audience member, it was the place to witness the "New Negro" music and dance scene. Most of the principal jazz musicians, singers, and dancers of the time appeared at the Cotton Club. These included Robinson, as well as Duke Ellington, Louis Armstrong, and Ethel Waters. Although the Cotton Club was a desired club and Robinson was becoming well known, he was barred from performing there for years because his skin was too dark.

As Robinson traveled the country on the Keith circuit, Harlem had become known as the "Black Capital of America." Robinson moved to Harlem during the Harlem Renaissance, at a time when many other black performers and entertainers, like Scott Joplin and his wife, Lottie, were moving there, too. By then there were many venues for live entertainment and gambling in Harlem, both of which Robinson enjoyed.

When he moved to Harlem, Robinson treated it like he was moving to a whole new town. He immediately made friends with New York Police captain Edward P. Mulrooney, of the 132nd Precinct. He would often run into Mulrooney as he walked home early in the morning after a craps game. Robinson always deferred to his locality of Harlem, so much so that the mayor of New York City, Jimmy Walker, once remarked that Robinson didn't recognize the

The Cotton Club stood on the corner of Lenox Avenue and 142nd Street.

mayor of New York but thought him an assistant to Mulrooney. Later, because of his community involvement, Robinson would be known as the unofficial mayor of Harlem.

In 1928, Robinson and his second wife, Fannie, whom he had married shortly after his first marriage ended in 1922, moved into the prestigious Dunbar Apartments in Harlem. The Dunbar was a 511-unit complex between Seventh and Eighth Avenues and between 149th and 150th Streets. The complex was financed by the Rockefeller family. The rents were designed for tenants at the median income of $150, about $40 more than what the average Harlem family earned. Other tenants included W. E. B. Du Bois and his wife, Shirley Graham Du Bois, as well as Paul and Essie Robeson. Robinson's solo career was successful enough that he was able to afford the high rent. For as long as Robinson and Fannie were married, the Dunbar was their home base.

Robinson always prioritized the Harlem community. Throughout his career he performed in countless benefit concerts, many for Harlem's own organizations and relief programs. His benefits took on a crucial role in the 1930s, when Harlem was hard-hit by the Great Depression. Harlem was the home of more than two-thirds of all the blacks living in Manhattan in 1925. The population density was much greater in Harlem than it was in the rest of Manhattan. Landlords often didn't maintain their buildings. If Robinson saw a family being evicted, he paid their back rent and filled their cabinets with groceries.

FROM HARLEM TO BROADWAY AND BACK

The first all-black Broadway show, *Shuffle Along*, opened in 1921. *Shuffle Along* was famous for its all-black cast as well as its portrayal of true love between a black and a white character. The show ran for a full year and continued in revivals through the 1940s across the country. Despite the show's success, it was years before another similar show opened. Robinson hoped black theater would proliferate and ensure more rights for black performers.

By the late 1920s, vaudeville and Hollywood began vying for the same audiences. In 1927, *The Jazz Singer* with Al Jolson was released. It was the first talking picture, and Hollywood was beginning to look more popular than vaudeville. Robinson's manager, Marty Forkins, was concerned. If Robinson didn't expand onto Broadway, he might only have nightclub stages open to him when

The longest-running all-black revue to appear on Broadway was *Blackbirds of 1928*, starring Adelaide Hall.

the vaudeville circuit died down. At Forkins's urging, Robinson joined the cast of Lew Leslie's Broadway musical *Blackbirds of 1928*. The show had already been running for three weeks, and Robinson was set to star alongside Adelaide Hall. *Blackbirds* was the second all-black musical to open on Broadway.

Robinson had no expectation that the show would make him a star. *Blackbirds* had opened on May 9, 1928, at the Liberty Theater. Before he joined the cast, its first three weeks had been underwhelming. However, after he was cast, the weekly gross jumped from $9,000 to $27,000. The show continued for 518 performances, becoming the longest-running all-black show on Broadway.

Blackbirds contained many black stereotypes, like black children eating watermelon. However, it had a phenomenal singing, dancing, and acting cast. Despite the stereotypes, Alain Locke declared that it included true African heritage. Robinson appeared on stage only in the second act. His routine was very similar to his vaudeville act. He danced while singing "Doin' the New Low Down." The dance included tapping up and down a flight of stairs, his signature move. The audience loved it. All the reviews were glowing. At age fifty, Robinson had made it on Broadway. As Ethel Waters, a jazz vocalist and actress, wrote in her autobiography, "Harlem was crazy about Robinson. They would yell, 'Bo, Bo!' whenever they saw him ... Everybody in Harlem said Robinson was a magnificent dancer and they were certainly right." New York City dance and entertainment critics wrote about Robinson, claiming him as their discovery. With an all-black cast, Robinson finally had his big break on Broadway—at the height of the Harlem Renaissance.

Despite his success on Broadway, Robinson declined to go on tour with *Blackbirds*. He instead returned to vaudeville. While performing on Broadway, he had the unusual experience of going home to Harlem every night, and he missed the circuit. When he returned to the circuit, he primarily performed in New York

City and the East Coast. In fact, he was practically an artist-in-residence at the Palace Theater, where he famously debuted the stair dance.

In her 1934 essay "Characteristics of Negro Expression," Zora Neale Hurston wrote "to those who want to institute the Negro theater, let me say it is already established … The real Negro theater is in the jooks and the cabarets … Butter Beans and Sussie, Bo-Jangles and Snake Hips are the only performers of the Negro school it has ever been my pleasure to behold in New York." Although Robinson's breakout role may have been in *Blackbirds*, his reputation as a tap dancer and entertainer had already been established and recognized by other black artists in smaller venues. His performances in the vaudeville circuits, the Palace Theater, and countless clubs helped him become the most famous black dancer of the time and an ambassador of the Harlem Renaissance.

CHAPTER THREE
GAMBLING, MARRYING, AND FIGHTING

While Robinson was busy working the vaudeville circuits, he also met and married his first wife, Lena Chase. Robinson met Chase at her aunt's boarding house in Worcester, Massachusetts. Black entertainers generally stayed at boarding houses when they traveled because they weren't allowed in most hotels. At the time Robinson and Chase met, Chase was studying to be a teacher, a high aspiration for a black woman at the time. Robinson was ensconced in his partnership with Cooper on the vaudeville circuit. Robinson and Chase were married in New York City on November 14, 1907. They moved into Robinson's apartment on the west side of the city.

Unfortunately, their marriage was doomed from the beginning. The two spent approximately four months together before Robinson went on trial for a crime he didn't commit. After he was acquitted, he took to traveling the circuits again. Thus, the two spent very little time together and were never able to have children. They formally separated in 1916 and divorced in 1922.

Opposite: Robinson was incarcerated and spent time in Sing Sing Prison.

ON TRIAL

The trial involving Robinson occurred in 1908. Earlier that year in March, he had been arrested for armed highway robbery. Hyman Sussman, a tailor, accused Robinson of robbing him at gunpoint. After his arrest, Robinson was indicted on robbery in the first degree, grand larceny in the first degree, assault in the first degree, and criminally receiving stolen property.

Sussman had been Robinson's tailor for eight years and had made suits for Robinson over the years. However, Sussman insisted under oath that he did not know Robinson at the time of the crime. Prior to the incident, Robinson had given Sussman a $5 deposit on a $50 overcoat. That overcoat was stolen from the shop. According to Sussman, Robinson stole it. The night of the alleged crime, Robinson visited the tailor shop to demand his $5 because the coat was no longer available.

In Robinson's telling of the incident, he simply demanded his money back and had not been carrying a gun. Sussman handed Robinson $2 of the $5 and then began yelling, "Don't shoot me!" Upon hearing the shouts, a nearby shop clerk and a barber restrained Robinson until the police arrived.

Robinson went on trial on September 8, 1908. Although he was innocent of the crime, he never took the trial seriously and his attorney did not defend him well. The fact that he was not in possession of a gun and that he knew Sussman prior to the incident were not presented in the trial. No character witnesses were called on Robinson's behalf, and no supportive evidence was offered. After very little deliberation, the jury found him guilty. Robinson was sent to **Sing Sing**, a correctional facility 30 miles (48 km) north of New York City. Robinson was shocked by the verdict. From his perspective, Sussman was clearly lying. He believed the lies would be obvious to the judge and jury. Robinson was unaware that he needed to provide witnesses who could testify on his behalf; his attorney did not provide the necessary counsel to call such witnesses.

When Robinson was sent to Sing Sing, his partner, George Cooper, realized he needed to step in and help him. Because Robinson was in prison, Cooper had to cancel their performances. He lost out on countless performance opportunities and a regular paycheck. Cooper found new attorneys to look into Robinson's case. The lawyers requested a new trial and collected affidavits attesting to Robinson's own good character. One such affidavit came from Edward F. Albee, the manager of B. F. Keith Theatrical Enterprises (the Keith circuit). Albee's affidavit included a request to appear at the new trial and testify on Robinson's behalf. Bert Williams, George Walker, and countless theater and circuit managers signed similar affidavits. The attorneys also obtained affidavits from individuals who could testify to Robinson's and Sussman's relationship. They were not strangers at the time of the incident and had been acquainted for at least six years. Cooper's affidavit in particular attested to the fact that Robinson had been on the road at the time the overcoat was supposedly stolen from the shop.

In December 1908, a judge granted Robinson a new trial. The trial ended up being more of a tribute to Robinson than an actual court proceeding. Everyone who had previously submitted an affidavit testified to his dependability and good character. Another witness testified to his own difficulty getting a deposit returned from Sussman on a different occasion, revealing Sussman's bad character. The jury deliberated for fifteen seconds before acquitting Robinson. Shortly after the trial, Sussman was indicted for perjury. Robinson never publically mentioned his arrest or trial again.

FANNIE "LITTLE BO" ROBINSON

Robinson met his second wife, Fannie Clay, in a pharmacy on the south side of Chicago. Although he had a residence in Harlem, Chicago operated as a headquarters for Robinson's show as he traveled the vaudeville circuits. At the time he met Clay, she was studying to be a pharmacist at the Illinois School of Pharmacy. Originally from Tennessee, Clay was twenty years younger than Robinson. She was ambitious and believed that theater people were trash—and vaudevillians even more so. She was a hard worker, attending class during the day, working at the pharmacy in the evening, and writing papers and completing other schoolwork through the early morning hours. She was not looking to meet a husband at the pharmacy.

The first time Robinson and Clay had a conversation, Robinson asked to borrow money. He frequented the Walgreen's pharmacy at Thirty-Fifth and State Streets in Chicago because it included an ice cream parlor. He often ate up to 2 gallons (7.6 liters) of vanilla ice cream in a day. The store's supervisor was also willing to lend him money. One day, Robinson visited the shop to ask for money for a stake in a game. The supervisor was not there. Instead, he asked Clay for the money. He promised her repayment and a gift. Clay, for whatever reason, gave him the money. A month later, he repaid her. From then on, Robinson sought her out at the pharmacy whenever he was in town.

After the two were acquainted and had been flirting for a while, Robinson stole a diamond hairpin from her. He pawned the pin to stake himself into a game. A few days after the game, Robinson bought the pin back from the pawnshop and returned it to Clay, admitting his guilt. She was angry and let Robinson know it. Their relationship might have ended there. Instead, Clay took Robinson under her wing and suggested he open a bank account. At the time, he was making $100 to $200 a week. Despite the relatively large sum of money for the time, he was unable to

Fannie Clay supported Robinson through many setbacks.

Gambling, Marrying, and Fighting

save any money. At the age of forty, Robinson had never had his own savings account. To appease Clay, he agreed to send part of his salary to her, and she would deposit it in the savings account. Clay was one of the few people who had ever taken an interest in Robinson without wanting something in return. Not long after she opened the savings account, Robinson asked her for money again. He had pawned all of his possessions, including the suits he performed in, for a stake in a game. Clay decided to give him the money she had saved for her tuition. She also stood by him when, after showing him the total in his savings account, he spent it all over the next twenty-four hours.

Although Robinson's gambling often put Clay in a difficult position, she knew that he didn't spend all of his money gambling. She recognized that Robinson was generous to a fault. He often gave money away to any friend or acquaintance who he thought needed it more than he did. She also recognized the good and the bad in Robinson from the very beginning. When Robinson complained that their expensive long-distance phone calls were a reason to get married, Clay accepted it as a bona fide marriage proposal. She gave up her dream of being a pharmacist and owning her own drug store to become Robinson's wife and supporter.

Robinson and Clay's exact wedding date is not known. Although Robinson separated from Lena Chase in 1916, they did not officially divorce until 1922. It seems that within days of the divorce, Robinson and Clay were married. Robinson did not want his fans to read that he divorced one week and then got married the next, so there are many contradictory statements about when the actual ceremony took place. Most sources agree that Clay became Mrs. Robinson in St. Paul, Minnesota, in early 1922. From the time she said "I do" onward, she was known as "Little Bo."

Big Bo and Little Bo were opposites in many respects, but they were both used to fighting racism and discrimination in pursuit of their careers. Clay chose to go to pharmacy school to advance herself and her race. In the early 1920s, very few Americans

HIGH STAKES

Robinson was nearly as famous for his gambling as he was for his dancing. Throughout his three marriages, he never curbed his gambling habit. Going out on tour allowed Robinson to gamble and play pool or cards all over the country.

When Robinson was partnered with Cooper, he had the habit of drawing on both his and Cooper's pay to gamble. He would draw money from the box office after a successful matinee as a way to set himself up in a game. In one instance, Robinson rolled the dice for a $150 marker and lost. To make his marker good, he pawned his steamer trunks, clothes, shoes, and essentially all of his possessions, which he needed for his tour. In the end, Fannie Clay bailed him out with her tuition money.

Other performers that Robinson regularly toured with loved him and his personality. They did not, however, enjoy being asked for money. Rae Samuels, a fellow performer and the wife of Robinson's manager, Marty Forkins, was regularly asked to loan Robinson $500.

Many friends and acquaintances accepted Robinson's gambling. Because he was a gambler, incidents like the stock market crash didn't bother him. His carefree attitude toward money meant that he was generous, nearly to a fault. His general philosophy was that if he had money, it was there to be spent.

Big Bo and Little Bo dance together in 1939.

sought higher education. Even fewer were black. Clay was used to being the only black person in a white world. As one of the first solo black performers on the vaudeville circuit, Robinson also knew what it felt like to be the only black person. He often had to demand the same treatment that other white performers took for granted. Clay likely recognized that Robinson had the power to make a difference for future black generations. She was ready to join him in the fight.

Although Clay and Robinson eventually divorced, they maintained a good relationship. Robinson married again, but history remembers Fannie Clay as "Little Bo" and Robinson's wife. She had a great influence on his career, and in 1953 she wrote an article about their marriage in *Ebony* magazine, further preserving Robinson's legacy.

ELAINE PLAINES ROBINSON

In 1944, Robinson married for the third time. His third wife was Elaine Plaines, a chorus line dancer at the Apollo Theater. Her stage name was Sue Dash. Her sister, Dot, was a dancer at the Cotton Club, where Plaines and Robinson met. Plaines was nineteen years old and extremely shy. She was not sure what Robinson saw in her. Robinson, forty years her senior, was drawn to her despite still being married to Fannie Clay. He tried to be discreet about their relationship. When he wanted to take Plaines out to dinner, he also invited the entire chorus of *The Hot Mikado*—the 1939 Broadway show in which Robinson starred. In fact, he had gotten Plaines a role in the show. Eventually, Clay realized that Robinson was obsessed with Plaines, and she demanded a divorce. To her surprise, Robinson acquiesced and granted the divorce. Six months after the divorce was final, he married Plaines, on January 27, 1944, at St. Paul's Methodist Church in New York City.

Robinson was very close to Plaines's family, and in some ways it seemed he had married her for her family. Although he would

Robinson poses for a photo with his third wife, Elaine Plaines, on their wedding day.

never retire from dancing, it might have been his way of settling down. He still had his apartment at the Dunbar in Harlem, but Plaines's family lived in Brooklyn, and it became his home base. He called Plaines's mother "Mother," and he was interested in his sister- and brother-in-law. Plaines accepted his gambling, just as Clay had, but having family around helped him slow down a bit. Robinson began to take vacations, and Plaines persuaded him to stop working each year when he had earned $60,000. Their marriage ended with Robinson's death in 1949. They were married for about five years.

A FUNERAL FOR A LEGEND

Robinson's funeral was paid for by his friends and admirers. They started collecting funds when he was admitted to the hospital on November 14, 1949. He died shortly after Thanksgiving, on November 25, 1949. The funeral was supposed to have been at the Abyssinian Baptist Church in the heart of Harlem, but it had to be moved because of the large crowds expected to pay tribute to Robinson. His body was moved to the 369th Regiment Armory, just outside Harlem. Unfortunately, the change was not well publicized. When Robinson's body arrived, only fifty people were waiting. Eventually, the information traveled and the crowds arrived. It took two days for everyone—over thirty-two thousand people—to file past Robinson and pay their respects.

The funeral itself was also crowded, with over thirteen thousand people attending and only three thousand able to sit in the church. It was a who's who of show business. Jimmy Durante, Jackie Robinson, Bob Hope, Joe DiMaggio, Cole Porter, Joe Louis, Duke Ellington, and Irving Berlin were among the honorary pallbearers. Ed Sullivan planned and orchestrated the entire funeral. Adam Clayton Powell Jr., a member of the US House of Representatives and pastor of the Abyssinian Baptist Church in Harlem, spoke during the service. He summarized Robinson's

The marquee at the Palace Theater in the late 1940s advertises a vaudeville opening.

life: "Born within the shadow of slavery and dying at the middle of the twentieth century, the most glorious century of mankind, Bill Robinson was a legend ... He was a legend because, though he was an artist, he never missed an opportunity whether seeing a little boy on the corner, or Shirley Temple in Hollywood, of teaching part of his artistry to someone on the way up."

After the funeral, there was a procession in which Robinson's body went from Harlem to Brooklyn. He was buried in the actor's section of the Evergreen Cemetery. New York mayor Paul O'Dwyer and the pallbearers marched on either side of the hearse. Across Seventh Avenue, on the Palace Theater's marquee, a banner read "So Long, Bill Robinson. His feet brought joy to the world." The funeral was the largest in New York City history and helped secure Robinson as a legend.

RACISM AND DISCRIMINATION

Robinson was born into a segregated society in Richmond, and throughout his life he battled racism. He never performed in blackface, a ritual expected of black performers. He also eschewed the "two colored" rule and performed as a solo entertainer, though that took careful planning on his part. Despite these milestones, the everyday reception of Robinson out on the circuit was not always pleasant or kind. Reviews and articles of Robinson's performances show how Robinson was critiqued because of his skin color, even by audiences who loved him. On October 18, 1921, a reviewer in the *Pittsburgh Sun* wrote, "Bill Robinson, not as black as the ace of spades, but a gentleman of color, nevertheless." For whatever reason, the color of his skin was of great importance to the reviewer. Around the same time, a similarly racist reviewer for the *Rockford Republic* wrote, "Bill Robinson does as many monkey shines as any colored entertainer." Comparisons to monkeys or other primates have been a way to degrade black people throughout history. There were occasional reviews that didn't address Robinson's color, but simply his ability to dance and entertain. Most reviewers, however, made sure to note that he was a *black* dancer and entertainer.

Robinson faced quite a few challenges when traveling the vaudeville circuit. The circuit provided him with train tickets, but he had to find his own lodging in each town. A white performer's itinerary listed a hotel in each city they were traveling to, such as the Radisson Hotel or the Baltimore Hotel. Robinson's lodging itineraries listed boarding houses or spare rooms. Even though boarding houses offered more accessible lodging, some had signs that read "No Negroes, Jews, or Dogs Allowed." Meals were easier to find but sometimes included the indignity of having to go to the back of a diner to be served.

Fannie Clay, in her 1953 article in *Ebony*, recounts an instance in which Robinson was traveling the circuit by train. A fellow performer, who was a white Southerner, was teasing Robinson. Robinson tried to let it go for a while—which was a challenge because he had a very quick temper. The white performer began to ask Robinson why blacks have such a wide variety of skin tones. He kept asking questions about why Robinson's own skin was so dark, and why his wife's was so much lighter. Robinson then explained that sometimes lighter-skinned African Americans were the children of rich, white plantation owners and slave women. For weeks, the performer didn't speak to Robinson, but Clay was proud that Robinson stood up to the white performer without violence.

Robinson fought racism through his ability to make friends with the police and by demanding fair treatment. Clay described Robinson's approach to race relations: "Bill didn't preach or rave and rant about race relations and discrimination, but he wouldn't take anything from anybody." Once at an all night diner, he ordered a full breakfast and was refused service. After trying to place his order a second time, Robinson pulled out his signature gold-plated, pearl-handled gun and was served. Eventually he was taken into custody, but he was soon released because he was friends

Segregation, including separate facilities such as restaurants and waiting rooms, was a reality for Robinson when he toured on the vaudeville circuit.

with the town's sheriff. At every town he traveled to, Robinson checked in and made friends with the local police chief or sheriff. Clay said Robinson loved the police and the police loved him right back. Whenever he arrived in a town, he would drive straight to the police station, place his gun on the counter, and ask for a courtesy card allowing him to carry it. These relationships saved him from being tossed into jail and possibly forgotten about after a misunderstanding, which could easily happen to a black man.

Robinson poses with Olympic athlete Jesse Owens after the runner's triumphant return from the 1936 Summer Games. Owens later gave Robinson one of his gold medals as a token of their friendship.

As a performer, Robinson knew he couldn't single-handedly change the way the South operated, but he did the best he could. Oftentimes he performed for inmates at prisons. If the prison practiced segregation, he would demand that black prisoners be allowed to attend his shows as well. He might also employ the opposite strategy. If he was performing for an all-black audience, he would request that whites be invited. An occasion arose in Dallas, Texas, where Robinson appeared at a centennial celebration at an all-white venue. Robinson approached the manager, acknowledged the segregation policy, but asked if some of his friends (prominent Dallas citizens who were black) could attend the show. The theater management agreed to let the friends attend the show. They were seated in an upper box, and at times, the audience paid more attention to the black guests in the theater than to the actual show.

There are countless examples of how Robinson fought against the inherent discrimination he encountered. He often faced unwanted comments about his dark skin and how he was an Uncle Tom. In addition to challenging racism, he had his own challenges with gambling. Today, he might have been considered a gambling addict. Despite his gambling problem and quick temper, he married women who accepted him in spite of the challenges. He easily could have alienated himself from friends and family, but something about his talent and magnetic personality made up for the gambling. When he died, his estate only amounted to $24,169.43, a small amount compared to how much he was making annually. But if a funeral procession of over thirty-two thousand people paying their respects is any measure of wealth, Robinson lived a very rich life.

The Work of Bill "Bojangles" Robinson

"Everyone knew Bill all over the world, but few knew much about him. Many misunderstood him, dismissed him as a clown, branded him an 'Uncle Tom' or criticized him as a showoff. I can tell you about the real Bill Robinson."

—Fannie Robinson

CHAPTER FOUR

THE PROFESSIONAL TAP DANCER

Bill "Bojangles" Robinson was a highly accomplished tap dancer. Tap dancing, an American style of dance, began in the 1700s. It has African, English, Irish, and Scottish influences, but generally the emphasis is on the African and Irish roots. At the turn of nineteenth century, tap dancing had been in existence for about fifty years. It began to take off with modern jazz and as the entertainment industry began to change. American audiences became interested in music and dance. Tap dance wasn't just for Broadway. It was incorporated into minstrel shows, burlesque, carnivals, vaudeville, radio, speakeasies, revues, and nightclubs. By 1928, it was even featured in motion pictures. Robinson danced nearly anywhere he could. Today, you can still see him tap in films. Robinson danced in many mediums and countless venues, but he is best remembered as a tap dancer wearing a derby hat and a tuxedo, dancing down a staircase with a smile on his face.

Robinson danced in a split-clog. The split-clog was modeled after an ordinary shoe. It had a wooden half sole about 0.4 inches

Opposite: Robinson performs with his most famous dance partner, Shirley Temple.

(1 centimeter) thick and a wooden heel. The wooden half sole connected to the leather sole from the toe to a point behind the ball of the foot. The leather connection helped with foot flexibility and therefore created a clearer tap sound. Robinson took pride in having clear taps. He danced so much he went through twenty to thirty pairs of shoes per year, despite taking meticulous care of them. He devotedly used the same shoe store, Aiston Shoe Company, for new shoes. He treated his shoes in much the same way a musician would take care of his instrument. The shoes were the key to his art form.

Robinson's dance style brought tap up on the toes, dancing upright and swinging instead of using flat-footed steps. Flat-footed tap dancing, practiced by such popular dancers as King Rastus Brown, had previously been the preferred style. The physicality of Robinson's dance was light, as opposed to Brown's heavier steps. Some critics identified Robinson's dance as the prettiest thing they ever saw accompanied with the clearest taps they ever heard. His ability to achieve swinging **syncopations** made his dance style superior to nearly all of his peers'.

While Robinson is forever linked with the stair dance, he had a strong repertoire of dances and routines. He did not invent specific dance steps, but he infused them with his own style. Among the steps included in his routine were the time step, a scoot step, a double tap, an old man's dance, and tapping with a Chaplinesque waddle, to name a few. Sometimes his dancing included storytelling or jokes that were perfectly timed with the tapping. Robinson also had an infectious smile, which many critics noted was a large part of his appeal.

THE STAIR DANCE

When Robinson introduced his stair dance in 1918 at the Palace Theater, it was a crowd favorite. However, no one knew how much it would define his career. According to some critics, the stair dance was the first tap masterwork of the twentieth century. As he danced down the steps flanking the stage, the audience applauded. The dance itself involved a different rhythm for each step, usually with a different pitch as well. When he used the stairs as a prop, Robinson broke conventions. Dancers previously danced along an imaginary horizontal line on the stage. Robinson used new space on the stage. Despite its popularity, he was unable to implement his new dance right away. Not all stages had steps, so he had to creatively modify stages and build his own portable steps.

The stair dance did not stay on the vaudeville circuit, either. Often the stair dance appeared in Robinson's Broadway shows and films. After he performed the stair dance in the musical revue *Blackbirds of 1928*, he filmed the dance on a blank stage. Robinson wore his signature three-piece suit and bowler hat. He performed five choruses and variations for the duration of the dance. The film was shot documentary-style with a stationary camera. It allowed viewers to focus on the steps and sounds of the dance without the distraction of an act.

Robinson was not the only dancer to perform, or even invent, the stair dance. King Rastus Brown was a staircase dancer who, around 1918, was incensed by the upstart who was stealing his dance. Robinson was not threatened by Brown. He believed the dance was his. The true inventor of the stair dance, however, was likely on the vaudeville circuit around the turn of the century. In truth, it was fairly common for tap dancers on the circuit to dance up and down stairs. Regardless, no one made the dance as famous as Robinson. The fact that Robinson had his own set of portable steps cemented his claim to the stair dance. He perfected the stair dance and brought a new level of showmanship to it.

By 1921, the stair dance was a standard part of his act. The steps themselves were so much a part of Robinson's act that he did not want other performers performing on stairs. Robinson even tried to secure a patent on his stair routine through the US Patent Office in Washington, DC. However, his application

THE BASEBALL FAN

In addition to tap dancing, Robinson was a talented baseball player and a backward runner. He played baseball for the National Vaudeville Association, or the NVA, on a team called the Black Rats. He played second base. While he was playing a game, he challenged another individual to a race: they would have to run backward, from left field to first base. Robinson won the race. It was the first of many displays of his backward-running ability.

Robinson was also an avid New York Yankees fan. In 1925, he took one week off to attend the World Series. It was one of the rare times he took time off from the vaudeville circuit, and it would be something he repeated in the following years. Robinson also combined his love of gambling with his love of the Yankees. Both interests paid off in 1932 when Robinson placed a bet that the New York Yankees would beat the Chicago Cubs in the World Series in four games. He took the six-to-one odds and ended up winning $12,000. The Yankees even invited him as a special guest on the train home to New York as they celebrated.

Robinson, number 25, races backward as another player runs forward.

was rejected. Eventually, he simply became so well identified with the routine that no other performer would dare to impinge on the dance. He even received a check for $1,500 from another dancer named Fred Stone with a note saying that it was a partial payment for the stair dance he had stolen. Robinson's stair dance, along with his ability to demonstrate his personality on stage, made him an unstoppable force on the vaudeville circuit.

BREAKING RECORDS IN VAUDEVILLE

From 1914, when Robinson began touring as a solo act, through the early 1920s, his demand on the circuits kept increasing. In February 1921, Robinson played the Orpheum circuit. The next month, he also joined the Keith circuit. He and his manager, Marty Forkins, had to manage multiple contracts and circuit demands. In April 1923, Robinson opened at the Palace Theater in New York City. Eddie Leonard, who had helped him out of Richmond, was also on the bill at the Palace. It was a momentous engagement. Robinson, however, still was billed second, a less-than-desirable spot. Despite his spot in the program, audiences and critics loved him. Forkins used Robinson's sometimes-unfortunate billing position to his advantage. Forkins took out an advertisement marketing Robinson as a performer who enjoyed the number two spot—saying he considered it lucky. As a result, Robinson was offered a new two-year contract with the Keith circuit. He would start after he finished his current Orpheum contract. Robinson had made history as the first performer to do a run of four consecutive seasons on the Orpheum circuit. By signing the Keith circuit contract, he was on his way to setting the record for twelve years of consecutive seasons on the vaudeville circuit. From 1914 to 1927, Robinson never experienced a layoff. He danced fifty-two weeks per year. By the end of 1923, critics were predicting that he would create a sensation as a star of a musical revue on Broadway.

BOJANGLES SINGS

When Robinson partnered with Theodore Miller at the Douglass Club in the early 1900s, their act was primarily dancing. Critics, however, noted his singing. In their act, Robinson sang "Old Uncle Eph," a popular song from *The South Before the War*. At the same time, Miller sang an entirely different tune. Robinson harmonized with Miller, or any other partner, regardless of what they sang. Early on, it was clear that Robinson was a talented entertainer. Whether singing or dancing, when combined with his personality, audiences were entertained and satisfied.

Even as his fame as a dancer grew, he continued to have success as a singer. In 1925, Robinson performed in Chicago with an entertainer named Nora Bayes. During the show, Robinson debuted a song titled "Your Lips Tell Me No, No; But There's Yes, Yes in Your Eyes." This number received a warm reception and became a fan favorite. Robinson performed it with Bayes, a white woman. Not only that, it was a love song performed to an audience of white ladies. Robinson's talent and charm were enough to make these points fall to the wayside. The song was continually requested as he traveled the circuits. Although Robinson's goal as an entertainer was not to fight for racial justice, his ability to entertain sometimes provided opportunities for change.

BACKWARD RUNNING

In 1925, Robinson had a hard time getting the spot that he wanted on the circuits. In fact, he was often unable to get the headlines he wanted. So, he chose to make the headlines and generate publicity in a different way. Robinson got top billing on the sports page. His "freak sprinting," as reviewers called it, otherwise known as his backward running, wowed the crowds. He could run backward faster than nearly any runner could sprint forward. He sprinted backward at the Olympic trials in Los Angeles and won the 100-yard

Robinson flashes his iconic smile in his headshot, taken circa 1920.

(91-meter) dash in 14.2 seconds. In Denver, he ran 75 yards (69 m) backward and beat the city's best sprinters. Most of Robinson's running exhibitions were staged while he was on the Orpheum circuit in the West and Midwest. Soon, the Keith-Albee circuit began to sponsor similar exhibitions in the East.

BOJANGLES IN DEMAND

Occasionally, Robinson got the big breaks in billing he desired. In 1925, the E. F. Albee Theater opened in Brooklyn. Albee selected the performers himself. He wanted the best of every type of act available. With that criterion, he selected Robinson as the one black act to appear on the opening bill. Robinson came on right before intermission. He had the honor of being the first big hit at the new theater.

Again, Broadway chatter began to increase. Robinson was continually mentioned as someone who should star in a Broadway revue. Carl Van Vechten, a patron and proponent of the Harlem Renaissance, was among those calling for Robinson on stage. Instead of going straight to Broadway, Robinson headed to Europe in the summer of 1926. According to his wife Fannie's scrapbooks, he played in London, Paris, and Venice.

Although critics called for Robinson on Broadway, he was satisfied with the vaudeville circuits. He knew the circuit and theater managers, as well as the police superintendents in every town. He didn't mind almost always being on the road. The vaudeville circuits were changing, however. The Keith-Albee-Orpheum circuits merged, forming a chain. They merged again in 1929 to become the Radio-Keith-Orpheum motion picture theater chain.

BOJANGLES ON BROADWAY

Joining the cast of Lew Leslie's *Blackbirds of 1928* was the perfect opportunity for Robinson, but it was a gamble for Leslie, who put nearly all of his money into the show. *Blackbirds* opened on May 9, 1928, at the Liberty Theater. Its first three weeks at the box office were underwhelming. It looked as if the show would have to close. After Robinson joined the cast, however, the weekly gross jumped from $9,000 to $27,000. The show itself continued for 518 performances, becoming the longest running all-black show on Broadway. Robinson's performance was similar to his vaudeville act. He sang "Doin' the New Low Down" and performed on a set of stairs. He cleverly watched his own feet as he danced, encouraging the audience to do the same. The technique worked. The audience was enraptured. Even though Robinson didn't even appear on stage until the second act, he generated more buzz for the show than any other actor. Years later, in 1933, Robinson joined the cast of a new edition of *Blackbirds* for a month.

While Robinson declined to go on tour with *Blackbirds*, his career had been changed. He began to make even more money. He became the top-paid black entertainer in the world. At the peak of his career, Robinson was making an estimated $4 million per year. Forkins booked him at double his vaudeville salary. Robinson was in demand for benefit concerts for a variety of causes. Though he wanted to continue his vaudeville circuits, Robinson recognized that at his age it would be easier to play primarily in New York City and the East Coast. By some accounts, he became the artist-in-residence at the Palace Theater.

Robinson starred in *Brown Buddies* as his next Broadway musical revue. His manager produced the show. *Brown Buddies* featured Adelaide Hall, who Robinson had starred with in *Blackbirds*. The show had minimal story and lots of singing and tap dancing. *Brown Buddies* received few good reviews. Robinson's performance, however, got rave reviews. It ran for 113 performances. After the closing of *Brown Buddies* in 1930, there were few opportunities for Robinson to appear in Broadway revues.

Musical revues with an all-black cast no longer had a strong draw for audiences. The Harlem Renaissance was losing momentum. Despite changing audience tastes, Robinson's fame was at an all-time high in the early 1930s. In fact, by the early 1930s, he was too big of a star to return to the vaudeville circuits. He could only play the Palace and other illustrious theaters. Although he was most comfortable on the vaudeville circuits, the time had come for him to switch mediums.

HOT FROM HARLEM

Robinson's popularity didn't immediately transfer to Hollywood. He and Forkins improvised to find steady work. They found a new avenue in the vaudeville musical revue. Using singers and dancers from his previous shows, *Blackbirds* and *Brown Buddies*, Robinson put together the musical revue *Hot from Harlem*. Most of the singers and dancers weren't in demand elsewhere. They performed the popular numbers from shows like "Still Goin' to Town." Robinson himself spent a lot of time on stage during the show, performing in multiple numbers. *Hot from Harlem* opened on February 13, 1932, at the Palace Theater. The show received glowing reviews and began to travel the country on the Radio-Keith-Orpheum (RKO) circuit. The show itself had some challenges. A fire at the Palace Theater required new scenery and costumes. In one performance, a rat came onstage, a scandalous event in a New York theater. Despite these hiccups, the show was largely a success.

After a year, the show's name was changed to *Goin' to Town* and the popular song "Stormy Weather" was added. The change in title signified how unpopular Harlem had become. Tastes had changed when Prohibition was repealed and the Great Depression set in. The Cotton Club and another prominent Harlem institution, Connie's Club, moved downtown. Harlem suffered and its residents lived in hunger, despair, and violence. Harlem was no longer en vogue. Robinson's career and fame had outlasted the Harlem Renaissance.

TRYING OUT HOLLYWOOD

Robinson starred in his first ever film, *Dixiana*, which was released in the summer of 1930. The film was an RKO release—a comfortable project for Robinson to choose. The cast was predominantly white. It starred Bebe Daniels and featured several comedians. Robinson had a specialty role as a servant. He performed his staircase dance and received praise for his performance. The film itself did not do well. In 1932, Robinson appeared in the first all-black film ever made, *Harlem Is Heaven*. It was a Herald Pictures Inc. production. The film played in northern theaters and southern churches. It got very little exposure and did very little to advance Robinson's film career.

The Harlem Renaissance ended with a riot in 1935. One-third of the nation's population was living in abject poverty. The 1930s and the Great Depression had changed the nation and the entertainment industry. Tap dancing was as popular as ever, but vaudeville was losing popularity. Hollywood and the silver screen stepped in to take its place. Despite the lean times of the 1930s, the period's movies were glamorous and filled with drama, music, and dance. Movies provided audiences with an escape from reality. Musicals especially brought elegance and happy endings to Americans whose lives were far different from what they saw on the silver screen.

ROBINSON AND TEMPLE

Shirley Temple was born in 1928. At the age of four, she began dancing for a series of one-reel comedies called *Baby Burlesks*. *Stand Up and Cheer* was Temple's debut film. She held a small role

Good friends, Robinson and Shirley Temple hold hands as they walk down the sidewalk in Hollywood.

The Professional Tap Dancer

where she sang and tap-danced. Audiences fell in love. By 1935, Temple was the number one box office star. She would hold this position for three more years. From 1934 to 1940, Temple made twenty-four films. Fifteen of them included musical numbers where she tap-danced.

After some hard bargaining by Forkins on Robinson's behalf, in November 1934 it was announced that Robinson would co-star with Shirley Temple in her next movie, *The Little Colonel*. The movie's plot was pretty standard for the time. The little girl, played by Temple, brings together her mother and curmudgeon grandfather in the **postbellum** South. The mother was previously disowned for marrying a Yankee. Robinson played a servant who danced whenever requested and comforted the little girl. The setting, a Southern mansion, had a grand staircase that was an ideal setting for Robinson's stair dance.

Robinson performed his signature stair dance, which he modified to partner with Temple. The scene became quite famous and was the highlight of the film, but it took a lot of work and patience on Robinson's part. He had to teach Temple the dance. He knew that it was too complex to teach a seven-year-old in just a few days. He had to look at his stair dance differently and find ways to feature Temple. The two teaming up on the dance had a phenomenal effect. Temple didn't perform the most complex steps, but Robinson used Temple's taps to create complimentary sounds.

By September 1935, the next Robinson and Temple film was in the works. *The Littlest Rebel* was set in the South during the Civil War. The mother character dies and Yankees invade the mansion home. They arrive during the child's birthday party and capture her father. The old family butler, Uncle Billy, played by Robinson, becomes Temple's guardian. Together they travel to Washington, DC, to ask President Lincoln to pardon her father. They finance their trip by dancing.

The Littlest Rebel was a unique chapter in black film history. It was the first time that a black person was responsible for a white life in film. Audiences trusted that Uncle Billy would keep the little girl safe because he was articulate and reliable. These are characteristics that weren't often given to black characters. The genuine chemistry between Robinson and Temple helped make the film successful. Though Robinson's acting was not praised, his dancing was.

His films with Shirley Temple opened up opportunities for Robinson to appear in other films. Here, Robinson performs with Will Rogers in the 1935 film *In Old Kentucky*.

OTHER FILM ROLES

The Little Colonel launched Robinson's film career, but that didn't necessarily mean he was always in demand as an actor. Few dramatic roles were available for black actors. Robinson made his way by doing specialty numbers in various films. Some of the films he danced in included *Hooray for Love* (1935) and *The Big Broadcast* (1937). Robinson had a bigger role as Will Rogers's servant in *In Old Kentucky* (1935). In that film, Robinson teaches his employer how to dance. The narrative also included a subplot on the history of tap. In the end, with Robinson's help, Rogers escapes from prison by putting on blackface and imitating Robinson's dancing. *One Mile from Heaven* (1937) was Robinson's first true dramatic role. He played a police officer, but still managed to get a dance into the film. The film didn't do well at the box office. After *One Mile from Heaven*, Robinson filmed *Rebecca of Sunnybrook Farm*, another film with Shirley Temple.

MORE OPPORTUNITIES IN NEW YORK

In 1936, Robinson proudly accepted the unique opportunity to perform at the opening of the new downtown Cotton Club. With 80 percent of Harlem residents accepting public assistance by 1934, Harlem was no longer an exotic location that rich Manhattanites wanted to visit. Race tensions rose between white Harlem storeowners and black residents. Harlem residents were up in arms. They could not get jobs at the stores, and they could not afford to buy things from the stores. Owners of the Cotton Club chose to move the venue to a more desirable part of Manhattan.

As the top black entertainer in the world, Robinson was a must-have for the Cotton Club. Previously, he had not been invited to play at the club because his skin was too dark. But for the

Robinson played the emperor in *The Hot Mikado*.

opening, Robinson shared top billing with Cab Calloway. Another 130 performers joined in the celebration. Robinson introduced a new dance called "The Suzi-Q." In fourteen weeks, the Cotton Club made $500,000 with its reopening show.

THE HOT MIKADO

Robinson also starred in the Broadway musical *The Hot Mikado*, which debuted in New York in 1939. The show was based on Gilbert and Sullivan's *The Mikado* but with **swing** music. It had a cast of over fifty people, many of whom were regulars at the Cotton Club. Aside from the orchestra, it was an all-black show. It opened on March 23, 1939, to a crowd full of celebrities. New York State governor Thomas E. Dewey and FBI director J. Edgar Hoover were among those in attendance. In addition, several battalions of uniformed police attended the premiere to support Robinson. They were not there to protect Dewey and Hoover, as many had assumed.

Robinson was cast as the star, the emperor. He wore gold lamé and gold tap shoes. He told jokes, sang, and did several dances. The showstopper was his rendition of "My Object All Sublime." The theater audience had enough applause and appreciation for eight encores. Although the popularity of tap dance was beginning to decline, some critics say Robinson was at his best in *The Hot Mikado*.

When the 1939 World's Fair came to New York, Robinson kept busy. He kept up a grueling schedule that summer. *The Hot Mikado* moved to the World's Fair grounds and Robinson performed out in Long Island. He then took the train back into Manhattan and performed 12:30 a.m. and 3:30 a.m. shows at the Cotton Club. Despite his fame, Robinson was not slowing down. He continued on Broadway for two more shows. In 1940 he performed in a white musical titled *All in Fun* and in 1945 he appeared in *Memphis Bound*. Neither show earned much critical acclaim.

RADIO AND TELEVISION

Robinson was one of the few black performers to successfully move up the entertainment ladder. He went from a pickanniny to a duet in vaudeville. From there, he moved from a single entertainer in vaudeville to Broadway, then on to Hollywood, radio, and television. Robinson, beginning in 1936, began reaching audiences that had never seen him dance in vaudeville, on Broadway, or in films. The sounds of his taps were enjoyed over the radio. A lot of the vaudeville gags he employed, such as making funny noises with his lips, complimented the tapping as well. On radio shows, Robinson also used his one-liners like "Everything is **copasetic**!" or "I haven't been this proud since I was colored." Robinson never fully enjoyed performing on the radio, or even on television for that matter. On the television, audiences wanted to tune in every week to see Bojangles dance a new dance. Although he might perform multiple shows in one day, he didn't have the same audiences coming back night after night. When he returned to a town on the circuit, time would have passed since his last performance. For all his fame and acclaim, Robinson had a limited number of dances and routines. His work as an entertainer was to perfect the dances and routines he knew and loved.

Chapter Five
The Famous Black Entertainer

Although Robinson had the stage presence and sheer talent that audiences ate up, his gigs required a lot of planning and preparation and what we commonly refer to today as public relations. His preparations were even more necessary because he was a black man. Audiences and venues unfamiliar with his work had to be persuaded to give him a chance. This was especially true when he began touring as a solo entertainer. Another vaudeville performer, U. S. Thompson, argued that Robinson's fame had nothing to do with public taste or race. It was his non-stop, can-do personality that made the difference. Thompson declared, "Bill Robinson had sense enough to get out on the streets and run backward and all that stuff. And fight and raise hell and then send the sheriff tickets. Box office: No other dancer was a public relations man like he was." Robinson recognized that no matter how much talent he had, audiences needed to like him to keep him in demand.

Opposite: Robinson celebrates his sixty-first birthday on West Sixty-First Street.

HIGH STANDARDS

Robinson's professionalism was notorious. He would go into a rage if other performers made noise while he and Cooper performed on stage. As a solo performer, his temper and expectation of off-stage silence continued. Later in his career, Robinson even fined performers if he didn't approve of their behavior. He did not tolerate rudeness in the audience either. Sometimes he stopped his routine and threw the offending audience member out of the venue.

Robinson held himself to high standards, as well. He put the same effort into a performance in remote Duluth, Minnesota, as he did for the esteemed Palace Theater in New York. Robinson constantly practiced his steps, even steps he had been doing for years, often at late and odd hours due to his sometimes-strenuous schedule.

While he never considered his high standards a problem, his fellow performers did not always take kindly to them. For example, Robinson never booked shoddy musical accompaniment. Rae Samuels, a good friend of Robinson's and the wife of his manager, described him as loving good musicians and personally disliking the bad musicians. Robinson was deeply offended by poor musicians. Ironically, despite his demands for perfection, he was unable to read his own music to learn his parts. He instead depended on his wife. The only way he could learn his lines was to have Fannie Clay read them to him until he was able to commit them to memory. He could learn a new song by listening to it twice.

AIMING FOR THE TOP SPOT

Robinson quickly worked his way up on vaudeville circuit. His quick ascension showed that audiences appreciated his acts. Once he was hitting the Keith and Orpheum circuits as a solo performer, he constantly strove for better billing.

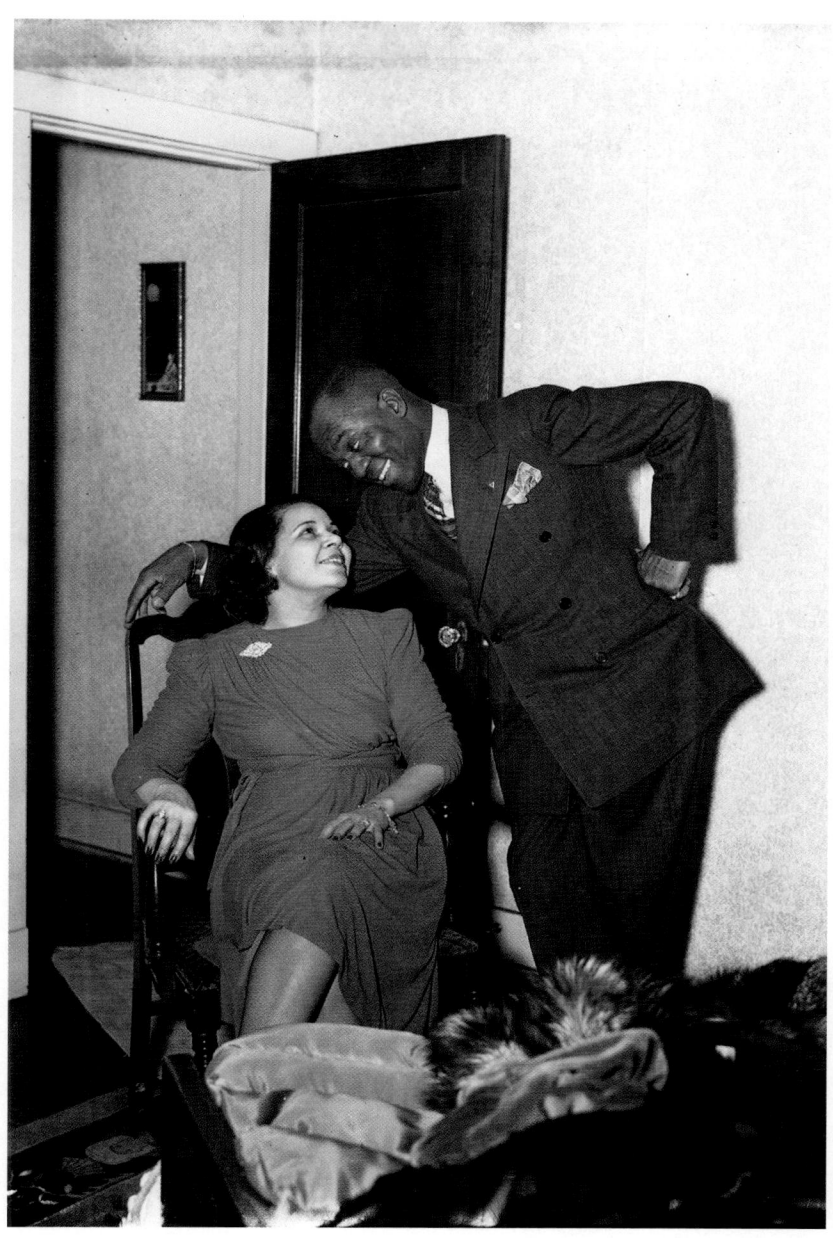

Fannie Clay, Robinson's second wife, helped Robinson learn his lines and music for different performances.

A SHORT FUSE

Robinson's temper was nearly as famous as he was. His childhood friend Eggie recognized his temper but attributed it to Robinson having been abandoned by his parents. He never grew out of it, however. Robinson's ability to "crack" got him into many fights. He had a growing tally of knife and razor lacerations in addition to bullet wounds. Over the years, he forgot how he received many of the scars because there were so many incidents.

Robinson's temper flared up often over racial indignities and injustices. He tried to be mindful of how a situation could escalate, but to ensure justice, he would often pull out his gun. One time, some fellow black entertainers were on the road in Sioux Falls, South Dakota, during a blizzard and were denied lodging. Robinson stepped in to help. He arranged alternative lodging with the assistance of his gun.

Sometimes Robinson's temper could get him into scrapes. Robinson was driving in Los Angeles when a car cut him off. He jumped out to yell at the careless driver, a large, white football player. The driver responded with racial epithets, and Robinson hit him over the head with his pistol. Robinson was arrested, though eventually charges were dropped.

A vaudeville bill had eight acts. The position on a bill was critical to any serious vaudeville performer. The better the position, the higher the salary and the better the chance for high-paying bookings. The first spot was a throwaway act, something that didn't have music or dancing and allowed ushers to seat latecomers. The second and third acts were short sketches, usually ten to twelve minutes. The fourth and fifth acts were more popular performances, after which there was a break for intermission. The sixth act was usually the largest. The intermission allowed them to set up for a large act. It might contain moving parts and could be a musical act. The top spot on the bill came in the seventh slot. The act could last for up to forty minutes. This was the spot Robinson coveted. After this came the final, eighth act. This was usually a throwaway number, often with an animal, whose droppings necessitated the final spot.

Robinson was playing the Orpheum in Chicago in the summer of 1922 when he received his first top spot in the billing. His act was called "The Black Daffydil" and was described as "A Cloudy Spasm of Song, Dance, and Fun." Clay included the advertisement in Robinson's scrapbook because it was such a momentous occasion. Though he got the top billing at one theater, that didn't mean that Robinson would hold the spot as he traveled. The top spot eluded Robinson on the West Coast, where he traveled after Chicago. He was not as well known in the West, so when he arrived at the Los Angeles Orpheum, Robinson had to work twice as hard for publicity. To get exposure, Robinson did his standard two performances at the Orpheum, and then danced in three more shows at the Hill Street Theater. After three weeks of that schedule, Robinson was rewarded as the headliner in Los Angeles.

Soon after headlining in Los Angeles, Robinson headed to the East. In Baltimore, he was billed in the second spot. During his performance he was hissed at on stage. The hissing continued and Robinson kept dancing despite the disruption. Eventually, three well-dressed, upper-class women were asked to leave. The

The Capitol Theater marquee advertises Bill "Bojangles" Robinson performing alongside Luba Malina.

audience encouraged Robinson to continue. At the end of his performance he addressed the audience, saying it was the first time in thirty years that such an incident occurred. Robinson said that if such an incident should ever happen again, he would ignore such behavior. Because Baltimore was below the **Mason-Dixon Line**, it is likely he was hissed at because he was black. Robinson was reminded that however successful he was in his career, his skin color would always influence how some audiences received him.

Another reminder of his tenuous position on the vaudeville circuit came in early 1923. Although some critics believed Robinson would do well on Broadway, the positive reviews did not ever ensure him top billing on the circuit. In Salt Lake City, he was placed dead last on the bill. E. F. Albee, head of the circuit, placed him in that position because the local Mormons were known to be racist against black performers. Albee let Robinson decide if he was willing to perform in such a degrading position, but he took to the stage anyway. Robinson rarely passed up an opportunity to perform.

Forkins, Robinson's manager, continued marketing Robinson's good character and good nature to get him a better spot on the bill through 1923. After getting a good reception at the Palace Theater in New York City in the number two spot, Forkins took out a newspaper advertisement quoting Robinson saying that he considered the number two spot lucky. Robinson, as a black performer, couldn't demand the top spot, but Forkins was able to market him in a way that demanded respect. Robinson didn't immediately receive the number one spot as a result of the advertisement, but Keith Management offered him a new two-year contract. Robinson's career in vaudeville was a product of his excellent tap dancing but also his ability to engage in public relations. As his career grew, the need for public relations was always there. As a black man, Robinson had to give bookers a reason to give him an opportunity.

ROBINSON PERFORMING FOR HARLEM

As the Harlem Renaissance was heating up, so was the talk about whether or not Robinson should be dancing on Broadway. Carl Van Vechten, a music critic and photographer, paid attention to the black artistic community and wrote about it during the Harlem Renaissance. Robinson and Clay corresponded a bit with Van Vechten, who wanted to see Robinson more active in Harlem and on Broadway. The trouble with Harlem and many of its clubs, like the Cotton Club, was that they had a skin color

Taxis line up outside the famous Cotton Club in 1938.

rule. Robinson's skin was too dark for most clubs. Robinson did, however, spend a lot of time in the **Hoofers** Club. Hoofers was a place where black male tap dancers gathered to learn from and challenge each other. It was neither a formal club nor a destination for whites. Although Harlem was Robinson's home and community, he wasn't always welcome to perform in its venues. In fact, a lot of Robinson's performances in Harlem were benefits and charity concerts.

BROADWAY ACCOLADES

According to Robinson, he got his start on Broadway by way of a favor. He joined the cast of *Blackbirds of 1928* as a favor for the producer, Lew Leslie. He had no expectation that the show would turn him into a star. Leslie wanted *Blackbirds* to be a game changer on Broadway. Ever since *Shuffle Along* premiered in 1921, Leslie had wanted to create another all-black musical. *Blackbirds of 1928* was the second all-black musical. It boasted Robinson as a cast member and made a modest amount of money. The show created hit songs like "Diga Diga Doo" and "I Can't Give You Anything but Love, Baby." Robinson's own number, "Doin' the New Low Down," later became his radio theme song and was known as one of his signature routines.

    The critical acclaim Robinson got for his performance in *Blackbirds* was nearly unparalleled in his career. Richard Watts of the *Herald Tribune* wrote, "This veteran tap dancer is one of the great artists of the modern stage." Brooks Atkinson of the *Times* wrote, "The most accomplished tap dancing of the evening is exhibited by Bill Robinson on his pair of stairs." Countless other quotations could be plucked from newspapers showering praise on Robinson for his role in *Blackbirds*. At the age of fifty, the critical establishment declared that Robinson had "made it."

The Famous Black Entertainer

Bill "Bojangles" Robinson

Personally, Robinson didn't feel like Broadway was much different than vaudeville, though he was proud of his Broadway debut.

While *Blackbirds* with its all-black cast was a foundational success, it still contained a lot stereotypes. It did nothing to change how white audiences viewed black performers. Critics and audiences accepted black stereotypes. Most critics disliked the show's comedy scenes, but only one critic, Heywood Bround, objected to the portrayal of a black man as a shiftless, happy-go-lucky individual. Even the programs for *Blackbirds of 1928* contained cartoon versions of blacks playing poker. In one playbill, a photo of the chorus displayed a black child eating a slice of watermelon. The Baltimore *Afro-American*, a primarily black newspaper with little circulation among whites, printed a review in which L. K. McMillan praised the dancing but felt that the show itself was doing more harm than good for black people. McMillan's review was on point regarding the ideals of the Harlem Renaissance. The prevailing popular opinion, though, was that Robinson was phenomenal.

Robinson's performance in *Blackbirds* made him the most famous man in Harlem. This fame also had some negative repercussions. Robinson became the target for two kidnappers who made money through ransoms. Luckily for him, the men were arrested. After the kidnapping plot was revealed, Harlem's 132nd Precinct presented Robinson with a pearl-handled, gold-plated revolver to use for protection. Robinson felt that the gift was one of the greatest honors of his life. From the moment he was presented with the gun, he carried it with him nearly everywhere.

Robinson received so much praise for *Blackbirds* that his next Broadway musical, *Brown Buddies*, ran mostly off of Robinson's success. The show itself received a lot of adverse criticism in 1930, but as the headline dancer, Robinson brought in audiences.

Opposite: Bojangles Robinson's skill was so well known that he was sometimes called the King of Tapology.

In general, critics recognized the performers, Robinson included, as extremely talented, but with very little music to back them up. A review from George Jean Nathan declared that Robinson was not just a great dancer but an actor as well. By identifying his ability to act, this review helped Robinson be taken seriously in Hollywood.

Critics also complained that the black performers in *Brown Buddies* were copying white shows, and that they didn't show any innovation. Of course, an all-black Broadway show can't erase or rewrite the history of blacks on stage. All-black musical shows were often financed, staged, and directed by white men. They expected to see a certain interpretation on stage. Black actors had little control over their on-stage image.

The only other unequivocal Broadway success for Robinson was *The Hot Mikado*. The show originally had a hard time getting funded. In fact, no one would agree to fund the show unless Robinson signed on. By the late 1930s, Robinson was considered an entertainer who could guarantee success on Broadway—as opposed to the risk he was in the 1920s. Eventually, he did join the show and he performed the showstopper. His rendition of the song "My Object All Sublime" brought down the house. Because of its popular appeal, *The Hot Mikado* ran at the World's Fair on Long Island. Robinson's own popularity at the fair manifested itself when August 25, 1939, was declared Bill Robinson Day. In honor of the occasion, Robinson, who was always up for a publicity stunt, wanted to do a dance on the giant machine that counted the daily attendance. Unfortunately, the company that insured his legs held a $30,000 policy and decided the stunt was too dangerous. Instead, he did some of his famous backward running exhibitions in honor of his day at the fair.

ROBINSON'S HOLLYWOOD RECEPTION

On Broadway, Robinson was known for his professional and dapper image. He often appeared in a top hat and tails and was always impeccably dressed. When Robinson performed, he played a version of himself. He therefore controlled his own image in clubs and on the stage. There were few roles for black entertainers that granted them such autonomy and dignity. In Hollywood, he was constantly cast in servant roles and had to dress and perform as others requested. For Robinson, the greatest challenge in Hollywood was keeping his temper in check. He knew that if his image was ever tarnished on account of an outburst, it would not just affect him, but nearly every black person in entertainment trying to make something of themselves. He represented more than just himself. He was breaking down barriers by dancing in Hollywood.

Many of Robinson's Hollywood films were panned by critics but loved by audiences. Audiences had already fallen in love with Shirley Temple, and for most audiences, pairing Robinson with Temple was completely endearing. Their success was reflected at the box office. With his appearance in *The Little Colonel*, Robinson became a Hollywood standard, albeit one that had a hard time getting leading roles.

Robinson's workload was rarely steady when he was in Hollywood. For a while he freelanced and took on small roles in ensembles. Aside from Temple, Robinson never had a long-lasting female partnership. He generally performed as a star soloist, with one exception. In the 1935 film *Hooray for Love*, he danced with Jeni LeGon. LeGon was the only African-American female dancer ever partnered with Robinson in film.

Robinson's 1943 film *Stormy Weather* also did well at the box office, although it was panned by critics. The film used the revue format and even featured Cab Calloway's swinging big band. It was a romance story between a rising star, played by Lena Horne, and a mature dancer, Robinson. Horne sang "I Can't Give You Anything but Love, Baby" and "Stormy Weather." The film epitomizes the wartime escapism audiences wanted. By 1943, the United States was embroiled in World War II. Robinson's dance routines, although they were included in several other films, were just the comfort

that American audiences wanted. Although Robinson did well in the film, the real excitement of the film was due to the Nicholas Brothers' dance to Cab Calloway's "Jumpin' Jive."

THE HERO AND HIS MYTH

While critics generally tended to praise Robinson and audiences flocked to see him, his own black community was less sure of his greatness. His fellow black entertainers held especially complicated views of him. By the time *Brown Buddies* closed in 1930, Bill "Bojangles" Robinson was household name, but many black households did not see him as a hero. Robinson's success brought out jealousy, and his close relationships with whites were criticized. Ethel Waters, a jazz singer and actress, was suspicious of how well Robinson got along with white people. She also didn't think that he was that great of a dancer. Waters's criticism may have been personally motivated, however. She and Robinson never got along very well. In fact, when Robinson and Fannie Clay moved to Los Angeles, they named their dog "Ethel Waters." That way, they could yell, "Stop that, Ethel!" when it barked or misbehaved. Because Robinson was so successful, many assumed he had done something unethical to achieve such success. He was accused of having turned his back on black folks to receive favors from whites. It could be from this perception that he earned the reputation of "Uncle Tom."

Being an Uncle Tom means that Robinson would have always had to say "yes" to whites and act in a meek way. But this is not at all indicative of his character. Robinson had a strong personality, and he wanted things done his way or not at all. His temper could flare in an instant. This often caused other entertainers who worked directly with him to have problems getting along with him.

Opposite: This poster advertises the 1943 musical *Stormy Weather* starring Lena Horne, Bill Robinson, and Cab Calloway.

Robinson's loyalty to other blacks was often criticized, even as his fame continued to grow.

In addition, some question whether Robinson ever reached out to help younger, up-and-coming dancers. Within the black community, there was an unspoken rule that you needed to help your own community succeed. But if someone took a favor from Robinson, he might loudly proclaim it and embarrass the person in public. Rex Stewart, a jazz **cornet** player, explained how he thought the black community perceived Robinson: "Adored as he was by the white audiences of his time, Robinson was pretty hard to take among his own people, especially the younger ones." Generally, though, once a performer got to know Robinson, he quickly became beloved.

What few fans, black or white, understood was that Robinson had to travel increasingly in white circles. There were few other famous stars with dark skin in his same position—and even fewer black managers, producers, or directors who could give him work. This became even more apparent during the Great Depression. In 1931, two-thirds of Manhattan theaters shut down. It was reported that nearly twenty-five thousand theatrical people were unemployed. Of those twenty-five thousand, three thousand were black. Essentially, all the black performers and theater workers at the time were unemployed. Though the Great Depression hit Harlem hard, wealthy Manhattan residents didn't have to change their plans. Tap dancing was the "in" thing. When Robinson was in New York, he might spend an afternoon teaching tap to debutantes and then perform for the wealthy in in the evening. Many of his opportunities had to come from whites. Otherwise, he would be without work like the rest of the community.

NAVIGATING THE GREAT DEPRESSION

Robinson recognized that because he was the top-paid black entertainer in the world, he had certain responsibilities. While he was often criticized for making a big deal out of loaning someone money or doing them a favor, he helped support a great many relief societies in Harlem without any notoriety. Together, Robinson, Clay, and Marty Forkins organized benefits. Robinson performed in approximately three thousand benefits in his career. Ed Sullivan often felt bad about asking Robinson to perform because he had such a hectic schedule and was always performing in benefits. If Robinson was in town and available, he would always say yes to any benefit requests.

During the Great Depression, Harlem's 132nd Precinct kept a list of wealthy individuals to call when there was a particularly destitute family. Robinson was often called on to help. He might buy a bag of groceries, pay for a funeral, or take care of a sick child's medical bills. In addition, one of the biggest free kitchens in Harlem was run by the Cotton Club. Robinson often worked there and handed out groceries. Unfortunately, he eventually had to stop handing out food personally because recipients became upset if the famous Bojangles didn't hand them food.

In 1933, Robinson was named the "Mayor of Harlem." Although he had been acting as such on behalf of the community for years, he was officially given the honorary title. One of his most famous acts as mayor was saving Harlem's Tree of Hope. The elm tree stood on the corner of Seventh Avenue and 131st Street. Residents believed it was lucky to rub the tree's bark. The tree was sick, and when Seventh Avenue was widened, the tree was removed. Robinson managed to save the stump and then appealed to Mayor Fiorello H. La Guardia to have a new tree planted as part of a special ceremony. Robinson always advocated for his Harlem community.

Robinson kisses the Tree of Hope in a rededication ceremony in Harlem, alongside Mayor La Guardia.

The Famous Black Entertainer

BELOVED BOJANGLES

Robinson was criticized, often severely, for how he addressed racial injustices, yet he was often beloved for the simplest things. Over the years, he collected tokens of appreciation from all over the country. St. Clair McKelway of the *New Yorker* discussed many of them in his profile of Robinson in 1934. Robinson was a special deputy of New York County, complete with a special badge. Because he had been threatened by kidnappers, he was given a gold-plated, pearl-handled revolver. He was an honorary member of the Grant Street Boys Association and a special inspector of motor vehicles for the State of New York. Often he carried documents establishing his personal friendships with police chiefs across the country, in addition to his other membership cards. He enjoyed nothing more than dancing, but he also took great pleasure in the various ways he'd been honored and given tokens of affection.

FIFTY YEARS IN SHOW BUSINESS

When Robinson helped reopen the Cotton Club with Cab Calloway in 1936, his manager, Marty Forkins, organized a gala celebration of Robinson's fifty years in show business. The gala kept the reopening show going strong over the Christmas season and assisted the Cotton Club. It demonstrated just how famous and beloved Robinson had become. At the gala, Forkins reminisced about the old days of vaudeville. Other entertainers recreated monumental dances and moments in vaudeville history. They performed the **cakewalk** and the buck-and-wing dance. Others imitated the stair dance. Heavyweight boxing champs playfully boxed with Robinson. Other personalities paid tribute, and telegrams from Shirley Temple, Fred Astaire, Mayor La Guardia,

Portrait of Bill Bojangles Robinson (both individuals) taken by James Van Der Zee, circa 1930

and Darryl Zanuck, the president of Twentieth Century-Fox, were read. The tributes carried on for so long that Robinson didn't get called to microphone to speak until 3:45 a.m. He began to cry as he spoke. He declared that his success was because he always worked just as hard whether there were ten people in the house or thousands, whether he was in the Midwest or on Broadway. The gala demonstrated Robinson's effect on the masses and the love and respect between Bojangles and his fans.

CHAPTER SIX

TAPPING INTO THE TWENTY-FIRST CENTURY: BOJANGLES'S LEGACY

Bill "Bojangles" Robinson was responsible for so many firsts as a black tap dancer that it is hard to summarize his legacy. He was the first solo black entertainer to make it on the white vaudeville circuits. He was one of three black acts allowed to play at the Palace Theater in New York during World War I. At the peak of his career, he was the highest paid black entertainer. When *Harlem Is Heaven* was released in 1933, Robinson was part of the cast that could boast having appeared in the first all-black film ever made. When he debuted with Shirley Temple in *The Little Colonel*, he and Temple were Hollywood's first interracial couple on film. Other praise for Robinson includes his having "the cleanest taps around" and having the greatest "sheer tap dancing ability." On the stage, Robinson changed tap dancing and the entertainment industry for years to come. He left the world, especially his Harlem community, a better place.

Opposite: Robinson dances on stage before an audience of people.

FAMILY

Robinson never had a traditional nuclear family. He didn't have any children to follow in his footsteps—or tap shoes. Unable to father children, he instead stood up for other children and young adults who needed a parental figure. Robinson sponsored a boy named Jay Gould Cotton, a fugitive from Savannah, Georgia. At some point Cotton turned up in New York and Robinson paid his bail. He also guaranteed that Cotton would show up at his hearing. Cotton showed up at his hearing wearing a brand new outfit, courtesy of Robinson. Another time, Robinson took in a boy named Roy Wright in 1938. Wright was a "Scottsboro Boy" who had been arrested in 1931 on charges of raping two white women. The case gathered national attention. Wright, with the help of the **NAACP**, won a new trial in 1937. He was released along with three others who were accused of involvement. Robinson paid for Wright's vocational training and other necessities, and he even gave Wright a place to stay. Robinson always took a special interest in young men who were unjustly arrested. Whenever he found himself in Brooklyn on a Monday morning, he would visit the local police station and sit in on the lineup. If he thought someone didn't look like he belonged there, Robinson would bail him out. In 1941, Robinson also became a wartime foster father for a twelve-year old girl whose parents could no longer care for her.

HELPING HARLEM

Robinson's second wife, Fannie Clay, acted as the caregiver to his legacy. In 1953, she wrote an article about her and Robinson's marriage in *Ebony* magazine. She wanted to garner support to honor Robinson with a monument. Clay wanted the monument to be erected on Seventh Avenue near the St. Nicholas housing project. It would serve as a reminder of how Robinson had often

Mayor La Guardia (*center*) and Robinson (*right*) attend a ceremony in Harlem.

stopped to give aid to any family that looked needy. She wanted the Harlem community to remember those good deeds. In many ways, Robinson treated the Harlem community as a family. He cared very deeply about what happened to them—even when he spent much of his time in Chicago and touring the country. One Christmas, Robinson and Clay drove around delivering baskets of food to those who might not have a Christmas dinner. The evening before, Robinson had performed in six benefit concerts, and most deliveries required him to climb four or more flights of stairs. When they finished delivering baskets, they returned home with only bacon and eggs to eat—exhausted but with no complaints. Oftentimes, when Robinson delivered food or goods, he heard the phrase, "I knew you'd come with my basket!" Those kinds of responses instilled in him a sense of duty to take care of others.

Robinson also worked to give kids a place to play in Harlem. On a neighborhood corner on Seventh Avenue he'd seen a weed-strewn lot. He went to the city's Park Department to ask permission to clean it up and add swings for the local kids. Because of Robinson's fame and his interest in the location, the Park Department said they would do more. They cleared the ground, laid cement, and planted trees. The Rockefeller family actually owned the land, and eventually they donated it to the city. As a result of Robinson's initiative, neighborhood kids had a new park and five new jobs were created through the Park Department.

RETURNING TO RICHMOND

Although Robinson left Richmond, Virginia, when he was quite young, he returned to the city as often as he could. Whenever he was able, Robinson wired money back to the city for various charities and worthy causes. During one visit in 1933, Robinson met with his childhood friend Eggie and noticed that there was no traffic light at a main intersection. Upon closer inspection, he realized that there were no traffic lights anywhere in the black part of the town. The situation was unsafe for the local children. Upon his return to New York City, he wired $1,240.70 to Richmond to purchase four traffic lights for the intersection that grabbed his attention. One of the lights included a bronze tablet acknowledging Robinson's role in the project. Robinson's brother, Percy, assisted in the project as well. This is some of the only proof researchers have that the two brothers kept in touch.

ROBINSON'S PERFORMANCE ATTIRE

Robinson's presence on the traditionally white vaudeville circuits changed the entertainment industry. For example, he had a direct effect on what black men were allowed to wear when performing on stage. When Robinson first began performing with George Cooper, he had to play the buffoon. He often wore costumes and embarrassing outfits like tutus. Once he was a solo entertainer, he preferred to perform in tails, or formal dress coats. He became

Robinson prepares in his dressing room before a show.

DUSTED AND POLISHED

Once Robinson was in control of his wardrobe, he was meticulous about its care. He never trusted anyone else to take care of his wardrobe. He always personally attended to it himself. Even when Robinson employed a valet and a dresser later in his career, he wouldn't let them touch his clothing. His suits were always cleaned and ready for use. When the clothing was hung up, each suit was evenly spaced a few inches from the next. When it was time to pack up and head out on the road, he packed his trunks himself. One trunk held his suits and one trunk held his shoes.

Robinson's shoes were always polished and stored beneath dust cloths. He couldn't stand lint or dust anywhere on his clothes. Robinson took great enjoyment in brushing his clothes with a whisk broom to remove any lint. According to Fannie Clay, he even brushed the white socks he wore on the stage. Robinson was always careful to ensure he appeared impeccably dressed—the total professional.

obsessed with new, well-tailored suits that he could wear to perform. Once Robinson was accepted as an entertainer, he took care to keep up that polished image. Bunny Briggs, a tap dancer from the swing music era, was directly inspired by Robinson's dress. Briggs saw him perform for the first time at the Lincoln Theater and was shocked when Robinson walked out on stage in a tuxedo and derby. Briggs recalled his surprised at seeing a black dancer perform "like a gentleman that's walkin' down Fifth Avenue!" instead of in the standard bellhop uniforms. Robinson paved the way for other blacks to appear on stage in dress of their own choosing.

NEGRO ACTORS GUILD

Early in Robinson's career, he recognized that black vaudeville entertainers faced challenges that whites did not. For example, white vaudeville entertainers could belong to the National Vaudeville Artists association (NVA) and receive health and burial insurance. They also had the use of a clubhouse in Manhattan. Blacks did not have a similar organization, and they were not allowed to join the NVA. Robinson worried about what would happen to his fellow performers if they became ill or died and had no way to pay for their care or funeral. Robinson corresponded with several circuit managers and the secretary at the NVA, Henry Chesterfield, in 1921 regarding the issue. According to their correspondence, at one point Edward F. Albee seemed open to creating a black branch of the NVA. In the black branch, performers might obtain insurance but would not be allowed in the clubhouse. Chesterfield wrote that he was interested, but he laid out a lot of conditions. He wanted Robinson to do a lot of legwork as well as organize the black entertainers. Robinson did not have time for that amount of work, and Chesterfield was unwilling to help. For the next fifteen years, Robinson paid for funerals of fellow entertainers whose families could ill afford the burial costs. He would occasionally

Robinson receives an honor early in his career.

take up the cause for health care in the following years. Finally, in January 1937, the Negro Actors Guild took on the cause. They provided a unified voice for black actors as well as money to pay for funeral and burial expenses. In an expression of gratitude for Robinson's work in getting the guild up and running, he became the guild's honorary president.

FIGHTING SEGREGATION

Robinson was always described as a phenomenal dancer, but also as an Uncle Tom. His second wife clarified that "Bill didn't preach or rave and rant about race relations and discrimination, but he wouldn't take anything from anybody." Robinson famously insisted on integration at a Dallas venue. The story of his asking that his friends be allowed to attend his performance is well known—the black friends attended the show. What happened a few days later is more unique.

Robinson, an avid boxing fan, was itching to get back to New York for the heavyweight crown fight between Joe Louis and Jimmy Braddock. The train that he was supposed to take was segregated and it was also the slow train, with many stops along the way. Taking the slow train would mean Robinson would miss the fight. He casually told a Dallas bank president that he needed to get back to New York in a hurry. Robinson lied about the reason, though. He said it was to perform in a broadcast, not to watch a boxing match. The bank president was eager to assist. He called the stationmaster to arrange a drawing room for Robinson, Clay, and four of their friends. The group was escorted through the white areas of the station and onto the train. They expected the train patrons, many of whom were rich and prominent businessmen, to be upset seeing blacks in the white areas. Instead, everyone was delighted to see the famous Bill Bojangles Robinson. Robinson had told a small lie, but he had managed to integrate a train in the South—no small feat. Following the incident, Clay received a letter from their friends in Dallas. Three black police officers had been appointed to the black district of the Dallas police department. Their appointment was explicitly made in honor of Robinson.

As Robinson got older, he became even bolder about standing up to racism. He also had enough support within the white community that he was able to get away with it. In the 1940s, Miami, Florida, was an extremely segregated city. Robinson visited

Miami on one of his rare vacations. He was not even supposed to be in downtown Miami past eight o'clock. The city had a curfew for blacks, which meant they couldn't perform in nightclubs. Instead of abiding by the discriminatory rules, Robinson, along with the local chapter of the NAACP, organized a benefit for underprivileged black children in the city. The benefit was supposed to be all-white, but Robinson insisted that blacks be allowed to attend, and Miami's mayor agreed. During the benefit, Robinson danced with the mayor's daughter and taught her a few dance steps. The benefit was just one step toward equality for blacks in Miami. By the early 1950s, just a decade later, black entertainers like Lena Horne were playing in Miami clubs.

INSPIRING TAP DANCERS

Robinson inspired generations of dancers the moment he danced out onto a vaudeville stage. The Nicholas Brothers, Fayard and Harold, were a famous, dynamic tap-dancing duo a little younger than Robinson. Their parents led a vaudeville pit band, so they may have been predisposed to show business, but they were both inspired by Robinson. Fayard first saw Robinson perform a benefit in Philadelphia but was unimpressed. As it turns out, Robinson was recovering from having four teeth extracted. A while later, he saw Robinson's 1930 film *Dixiana* and was floored by the famous stair dance. Fayard exclaimed, "When I saw him in that motion picture, that did it for me, that's when I fell in love with him." The brothers began dancing professionally the year *Dixiana* came out.

From Robinson, the Nicholas Brothers learned that every dancer has his or her own particular style. They admired Robinson's ability to dance on his toes. According to Fayard, by dancing on his toes, Robinson could perform the simplest step and get a big hand for it. Robinson eventually taught the brothers one of his soft-shoe numbers. When he was dancing a benefit, especially at

The Nicholas Brothers perform together in 1947.

Madison Square Garden in New York City, Robinson would call the brothers to dance with him on stage. In 1937, the Nicholas Brothers even opened a new Cotton Club show to replace Robinson's while he was filming in Hollywood. The Nicholas Brothers were known as "The Show Stoppers!" to Robinson's "World's Greatest Tap Dancer."

Ralph Brown, while not as famous as the Nicholas Brothers, was directly inspired by Robinson as well. When he saw Robinson dance for the first time, he knew that he also wanted to be a tap dancer. Brown recognized Robinson's skill was in his small steps, and that he could do more with just his feet than any other dancer. According to Brown, Robinson was undeniably the world's greatest tap dancer. Brown once found himself in Boston at the same time as Robinson. During that visit, he watched Robinson perform five times in order to study his moves. Robinson's moves were so intricate that Brown got headaches while trying to figure them out.

Countless other dancers learned from Robinson's routines and style. When Gene Nelson, a tap dancer in the 1940s, began tap lessons, the first routine he learned was Robinson's "Doin' the New Low Down." Flash McDonald, another tap dancer who admired Robinson from his films, changed his entire style of dance after becoming enamored with Robinson's clear taps. Jeni LeGon, a pioneering female tap dancer, was also inspired by Robinson. She was especially impressed by what a good teacher he was. Her own career became historic when, in 1935, she partnered with Robinson in *Hooray for Love*. LeGon was Robinson's only black female partner.

SHIRLEY TEMPLE

Robinson's effect on Shirley Temple is undeniable. The two were fast friends, and Temple affectionately called him Uncle Bo or Uncle Billy. While Temple had natural talent, as a young child she was not a fully mature dancer. She depended on Robinson for a lot of instruction when they danced together. Robinson invented a hand-squeeze system to help instruct Temple. Three squeezes meant a good part was coming, one long squeeze meant she was doing well, and no squeeze meant they had to do the dance again. From Robinson, Temple learned to visualize her sounds. In a 1989 interview, Temple recalled, "Every one of my taps had to ring crisp and clear in the best cadence. Otherwise I had to do it over." In

Shirley Temple and Robinson dance together on set in 1937.

addition to the technical aspects of tap, Temple credits Robinson with helping her learn exhilaration and joy while dancing.

Robinson and Temple didn't just have a simple student-teacher relationship. Despite their very different lives, they were also friends. The very nature of filming a movie meant that the actors had a lot of free time waiting around. Temple and Robinson would often just hang out together. Temple knew of Robinson's enthusiasm for Joe Louis, backward running, and vanilla ice cream. Upon Temple's death in 2014, many posthumous articles reflected on her and Robinson's unique friendship and partnership.

TAP-DANCING INTO THE TWENTY-FIRST CENTURY

When Robinson became ill and went for care at Columbia-Presbyterian Medical Center, he received more than five thousand get-well letters from admirers and well-wishers. Even President Harry S. Truman wrote to Robinson, wishing him a speedy recovery. His funeral was equally monumental. Upward of thirty thousand people paid tribute to Robinson as he lay in state. The joy that Robinson created through his dancing was obvious from the sheer number of people eager to pay their respects.

The momentum for honoring Robinson helped found a group called the Copasetics on December 5, 1949. The Copasetics was a social and benevolent club of musical artists. Its members focused on tap dancing and were dedicated to preserving the memory of Bill "Bojangles" Robinson. The club's motto was "Everything's copasetic," which was Robinson's favorite expression. It was his way of saying everything was just fine. The club, which continued into the twenty-first century, was also a vital social force in Harlem. The Copasetics hosted boat cruises, annual balls, and charitable performances. The members were all active tap dancers, and they worked to make sure tap dancing remained relevant. However,

Tap dancer Gregory Hines carried on the Bojangles legacy.

Tapping into the Twenty-First Century: Bojangles's Legacy

they weren't always the most popular group. Tap dancing soon took a backseat to ballet and modern dance on Broadway. In the 1960s, members made a conscious effort to revive tap and continue Robinson's legacy.

Honi Coles, one of the founding members of the Copasetics, called the 1950s a tap dancing lull. Coles was directly influenced by Robinson, referring to himself as a "disciple" of Robinson's. Coles danced with the same technique as Robinson, up on his toes and moving naturally. He wrote a song and choreographed an accompanying dance about Robinson called "The Mayor of Harlem." Coles worked hard in the 1960s and 1970s to revive tap dance. By the 1980s, he was considered the master of the form. Despite certain lulls, by 1980, tap dancing was back on Broadway. Robinson's influence was alive. Coles, along with Gregory Hines and other Copasetics, performed in *Black Broadway*, an all-black musical revue in 1980. *Black Broadway*, *My One and Only* (another musical featuring Coles), and numerous other tap-based musicals were performed 9,386 times in the 1980s. Tap dancing was back!

Gregory Hines was like a reincarnation of Bill "Bojangles" Robinson. Robinson was the most beloved tap dancer of the first half of the twentieth century, while Hines was beloved in the second half. Hines grew up dancing at a young age along with his brother Maurice. After school, he spent a lot of time at the Apollo Theater with many of the Copasetics, including Coles. While Hines wasn't an original member of the Copasetics, he was part of the 1989 homage film *Tap*. He was also a part of quite a few musicals featuring tap dance in the 1980s. In 2001, Hines produced a film about Robinson, titled *Bojangles*, on Showtime. He acted in the role of Robinson.

Tap dance gained momentum throughout the 1980s and brought Robinson back into American pop culture. In 1987, Jim Haskins and N. R. Mitang published the first comprehensive Robinson biography. On May 25, 1989, President George H.W. Bush signed a joint resolution declaring May 25 National Tap

Dance Day. The resolution said that tap dancing exemplifies the American spirit, with its combination of African and European influences to create something unique. May 25 was also Bill "Bojangles" Robinson's birthday, making it an appropriate day to honor American tap dancing.

In April 2008, the American Tap Dance Foundation's Tap City Youth Ensemble paid tribute to the Copasetics, Honi Coles, and Bojangles Robinson. The ensemble included thirty-four multiracial and multiethnic dancers. The performance included "The Copasetics Song/Coles Stroll"; "The Mayor of Harlem" ; "The New Low Down," Robinson's signature number in *Blackbirds*; and the "Copasetics Chair Dance." Preserving Robinson's dances and legacy was still important to the tap dancing community. A year later, in August 2009, Ernest Brown passed away. Brown was the final founding member of the Copasetics and one of the last people who had seen and heard Robinson's unique, clear taps in person. In some ways, Brown's death was the end of an era. Contemporary readers and students of Robinson have an advantage over previous generations, however. With a simple YouTube search, you can see Bojangles Robinson and Shirley Temple dancing on the stairs. Robinson's legacy is just a click away. Tap dancing may not be the most popular dance form, as it was in Robinson's heyday, but within the past ten years, young dancers have still been inspired by Robinson and his legacy.

CHRONOLOGY

1868 Congress passes the Fourteenth Amendment, granting African Americans equal citizenship and equal rights.

1870 Congress passes the Fifteenth Amendment, guaranteeing suffrage to all male US citizens.

1877 Federal troops withdraw from the South, officially ending Reconstruction.

1878 William Robinson is born on May 25, with the given name Luther.

1892 Robinson breaks into show business when he joins the traveling show *The South Before the War* as a pickaninny.

1900 Robinson beats the *In Old Kentucky* star Harry Swinton in a buck-and-wing dance competition.

1903 Robinson joins George W. Cooper on the vaudeville circuits.

1907 Robinson marries Lena Chase on November 14 in New York City.

1908 Robinson is unjustly arrested for armed highway robbery.

1909 W. E. B. Du Bois founds the National Association for the Advancement of Colored People (NAACP).

1914 Robinson embarks on his career becoming the first black solo entertainer on the vaudeville circuits.

1917 The first phase of the Harlem Renaissance begins; the United States enters World War I.

1918 Robinson debuts his world-famous stair dance.

1921 *Shuffle Along*, the first all-black musical, opens on Broadway.

1922 Robinson marries his second wife, Fannie, in Minneapolis-St. Paul, Minnesota.

1925 Alain Locke publishes *The New Negro*.

1926 Robinson travels on the SS *Leviathan* to perform throughout Europe.

1927 *The Jazz Singer*, the first talking picture, is released.

1928 The Dunbar Apartments open in Harlem and the Robinsons become residents; Robinson stars in his first Broadway show, *Blackbirds of 1928*.

1930 Robinson's first film, *Dixiana*, is released.

1934 Robinson is announced as Shirley Temple's costar in *The Little Colonel*.

1935 The Harlem Riot on March 19 marks the end of the Renaissance.

1939 Robinson stars in the *The Hot Mikado* on Broadway and then at the New York World's Fair.

1944 Robinson marries his third wife, Elaine, on January 27 in New York City.

1949 Robinson passes away on November 25; his funeral draws more than thirty thousand mourners.

ROBINSON'S MOST IMPORTANT WORKS

BROADWAY

Blackbirds of 1928 (1928)
Brown Buddies (1930)
The Hot Mikado (1939)
All in Fun (1940)
Memphis Bound (1945)

FILM

Dixiana (1930)
Harlem is Heaven (1932)
King for a Day (1934)
The Little Colonel (1935)
In Old Kentucky (1935)
The Littlest Rebel (1935)
Hooray for Love (1935)
Big Broadcast of 1936 (1935)
Clean Pastures (1937, cartoon)
One Mile from Heaven (1937)
Rebecca of Sunnybrook Farm (1938)
Just Around the Corner (1938)
Up the River (1938)
Road Demon (1938)
It's Swing Ho—Come to the Fair! (1939, newsreel)
Stormy Weather (1943)

GLOSSARY

antebellum Before the Civil War.

billing The order in which performers appeared, like a program, on the vaudeville circuit.

bootblack A shoe shiner.

buck-and-wing An early style of clog dancing that combines a simple time step (buck) with a simple hop (wing).

cakewalk A strutting dance, popular at the end of the nineteenth century, that evolved from black American tradition.

copasetic In good order; Robinson's favorite phrase to mean everything was good.

cornet A metal horn, like a trumpet.

Great Migration The mass relocation for many blacks in the early twentieth century to the North from the South.

Harlem Renaissance A black American artistic and social movement in the 1920s and 1930s.

hoofer A tap dancer who concentrates on the percussive tap movements, not the upper body.

impresario A person who finances a play, opera, or musical act.

Jim Crow An offensive term from a black person; the term would become a stand in for segregation laws.

Mason-Dixon Line The border between the North and South, which still held cultural impact in the years after the Civil War.

minstrel show A popular stage show with song, dance, and comic dialogue usually performed by white actors in blackface.

NAACP Stands for National Association for the Advancement of Colored People; a national advocacy organization started by W. E. B. Du Bois.

pickaninny A black male juvenile who danced and sang to provide backup in a vaudeville act.

postbellum Occurring after the Civil War.

Reconstruction The period directly after the Civil War through 1877 when the South was occupied by the military.

sharecropping A practice where tenant farmers gave a part of each crop to the landowner as part of their rent.

Sing Sing A famous prison north of New York City.

soft-shoe A dance performed in a slow 4/4 time, originally with sand on the floor.

stop-time One note played at the beginning of each musical bar to keep time.

swing Style of music developed in early 1930s with medium to fast tempos and a lilting rhythm.

syncopation In music, a displacement of the regular accent of the beat.

tap dancing A percussive American dance form having English, Irish, and African roots.

Uncle Tom A caricature of a black man who is excessively obedient.

vaudeville Entertainment popular in the early twentieth century that includes a mixture of specialty acts.

FURTHER INFORMATION

BOOKS

Cripps, Thomas. *Slow Fade to Black: The Negro in American Film, 1900–1942*. New York: Oxford University Press, 1977.

Gottschild, Brenda Dixon. *Waltzing in the Dark: African American Vaudeville and Race Politics in the Swing Era*. New York: Palgrave, 2000.

Haskins, Jim. *The Cotton Club*. New York: Random House, 1977.

Lewis, David Levering, ed. *The Portable Harlem Renaissance Reader*. New York: Penguin Books, 1994.

Lewis, David Levering. *When Harlem Was in Vogue*. New York: Penguin Books, 1997.

Locke, Alain, ed. *The New Negro*. New York: Touchstone, 1997.

WEBSITES

Dancing with Gregory Hines
artsedge.kennedy-center.org/interactives/gregoryhines
This video shows Gregory Hines dancing and discussing tap and Robinson.

Drop Me Off in Harlem
artsedge.kennedy-center.org/interactives/harlem
This interactive website covers a myriad of artists and entertainers from the Harlem Renaissance.

PBS: Kens Burns's Jazz
www.pbs.org/jazz/index.htm
This interactive website about the Jazz Age was designed to accompany *Jazz*, a Ken Burns documentary.

Turner Classic Movies: Bill "Bojangles" Robinson
www.tcm.com/mediaroom/video/135937/Bill-Bojangles-Robinson-Comments-by-various-actors-A-TCM-Featurette-.html
Contemporary black actors discuss the influence of Robinson today, with links to videos of Robinson dancing.

BIBLIOGRAPHY

Blair, Elizabeth. "Shirley Temple and Bojangles: Two Stars, One Lifelong Friendship." *NPR*, February 14, 2014. http://www.npr.org/2014/02/14/276986764/shirley-temple-and-bojangles-two-stars-one-lifelong-friendship.

Dunning, Jennifer. "Ernest Brown, Last Member of Original Tapping Copasetics, Dies at 93." *New York Times*, August 25, 2009. http://www.nytimes.com/2009/08/25/arts/dance/25brown.html?_r=1&.

Frank, Rusty. *Tap! The Greatest Tap Dance Stars and Their Stories, 1900–1955*. New York: Da Capo Press, 1994.

Gates, Henry Louis, Jr., and Cornel West. *The African-American Century: How Black Americans Have Shaped Our Country*. New York: Simon & Schuster, 2002.

Haskins, Jim, and N. R. Mitgang. *Mr. Bojangles: The Biography of Bill Robinson*. New York: William Morrow and Company, 1988.

Hill, Constance Valis. *Tap Dancing America: A Cultural History*. New York: Oxford University Press, 2010.

Hurston, Zora Neale. "Characteristics of Negro Expression." In *The New Negro: Readings on Race, Representation, and African American Culture, 1892–1938,* edited by Henry Louis Gates Jr. and Gene Andrew Jarrett, 355–363. Princeton, NJ: Princeton University Press, 2007.

McKelway, St. Clair. "Bojangles I." *New Yorker,* October 6, 1934.

———. "Bojangles II." New Yorker, October 13, 1934.

Robinson, Fannie. "I Remember Bojangles." *Ebony*, February 1953.

Stearns, Marshall and Jean Stearns. *Jazz Dance: The Story of American Vernacular Dance.* New York: Da Capo Press, 1994.

INDEX

Page numbers in **boldface** are illustrations. Entries in **boldface** are glossary terms.

antebellum, 7

billing, 26, 62–63, 65, 72, 78, 81, 83
Blackbirds of 1928, **33**, 34–35, 59, 65–67, 85, 97, 115
bootblack, 12
Brown Buddies, 66–67, 87–88, 91
buck-and-wing, 12–13, 24, 26, 96

cakewalk, 96
Calloway, Cab, 72, 89, **90**, 91, 96
Chase, Lena, 27, 37, 42
Clay, Fannie, 9, 31–32, 40, **41**, 42–43, **44**, 45, 47, 50–51, 65, 78, **79**, 81, 83, 91, 94, 100–102, 104, 107
Cooper, George W., 27–28, 37, 39, 43, 78, 103
copasetic, 75, 112
Copasetics (group), 112, 114–115
cornet, 93
Cotton Club, 30, **31**, 45, 67, 72, 74, 83, **84**, 94, 96, 109

Forkins, Marty, 28, 32, 34, 43, 62, 66–67, 70, 83, 94, 96

Great Migration, 21–23

Harlem Renaissance, 21–24, 29–30, 34–35, 65, 67–68, 83, 87
Hines, Gregory, **113**, 114
hoofer, 85
Hot Mikado, The, 45, **73**, 74, 88

impresario, 17

Jim Crow, 10
Jolson, Al, 17, **18**, 26, 32

Little Colonel, The, 70, 72, 89, 99

Mason-Dixon Line, 82
minstrel show, **6**, 10, **11**, 12–14, 17, 26, 57

NAACP, 100, 108
Nicholas Brothers, 91, 108–109, **109**

Palace Theater, 29–30, 35, **48**, 49, 58–59, 62, 66–67, 78, 83, 99

pickaninny, 15, **16**, 18–19, 26, 75
Plaines, Elaine, 45, **46**, 47
postbellum, 70

Reconstruction, 7–8
Robinson, Bill "Bojangles"
   arrests, **36**, 37–39, 80
   backward running, 60, **61**, 63, 65, 77, 88, 112
   Broadway career, 21, 32, 34, 45, 59, 65–67, **73**, 74–75, 85, 87–88
   dancing style, 12–13, 57–58, 108, 114
   early life, 7–9, 12–15, 17–19
   gambling, 17, 40, 42–43, 47, 53, 60
   generosity, 31–32, 42–43, 94, 100–102, 105, 108
   Hollywood career, **56**, 57, 59, 68, 70–72, **71**, 75, 89, **90**, 91, 99, **111**
   legacy, 99, 103, 105, 108–110, 112, **113**, 114–115
   marriages, 27, 31, 37, 40, 42, 45, 47, 53
   name, 9, 12, 14
   race, 9, 24, 27–30, 42, 45, 49–53, 63, 71–72, 77, 80–83, 89, 91, 93, 96, 99, 103, 105–108
   reviews, 27–28, 49–50, 58, 66, 71, 73, 82, 85, 87–89, 91

stair dance, 14, 23, 29–30, 34–35, 57–59, 62, 66, 68, 70, 108
temper, 12, 14, 50, 78, 80, 89, 91
Vaudeville career, 21, 23–24, 26–30, 34–35, 58–59, 62–63, 65–67, 75, 77–78, 81–83, **82**, 89

sharecropping, 21–22
Sing Sing, **36**, 38–39
soft-shoe, 12, 108
stop-time, 24
swing, 74, 89, 105
syncopation, 58

tap dancing, 13, 26, 29, 34–35, 57–59, 66, 68, 70, 72, 74–75, 83, 85, 93, 99–100, 105, 108–110, 112, 114–115
Temple, Shirley, 49, **56**, 68, **69**, 70–72, 89, 96, 99, 110, **111**, 112, 115

Uncle Tom, 10, 27, 53–54, 91, 107

vaudeville, 10, 17–18, 21, 24, 26–29, 32, 34–35, 37, 40, 45, **48**, 50, 57, 59–60, 62, 65–68, 75, 77–78, 81–83, 85, 96, 99, 103, 105, 108

ABOUT THE AUTHOR

Meghan Engsberg Cunningham received her BA in English and American Studies from St. Norbert College and her MA at the University of Wisconsin–Milwaukee. She completed her master's degree thesis on Charles Chesnutt's novel *The Marrow of Tradition* along with the texts that were precursors to the Harlem Renaissance. Meghan has spent time working with student writing as a writing center tutor at St. Norbert College and then as an Assistant Coordinator at the UW–Milwaukee Writing Center. She currently works in financial litigation. Meghan lives in Milwaukee with her husband, Stephen. Together they enjoy reading, running, and traveling.